CHASING THE WOLF

NATHAN SINGER

BLEAK HOUSE BOOKS

MADISON | WISCONSIN

Published by Bleak House Books, an imprint of Big Earth Publishing

953 E. Johnson St.

Madison, WI 53703

ISBN 1-932557-14-8

LOC 2005936200

Jacket design and cover illustration: Peter Streicher

Book design: Peter Streicher

for simon

THEN, OUT OF THE BLUE, THIS GIGANTIC *man appeared on stage. He glared out into the audience with his eyes rolled up like he was possessed ... hypnotized ... something ... The veins in that man's neck bulged and throbbed. His massive fists clenched. Lips locked, eyelids now locked. Jaw locked. A polytonal hum began to vibrate through the speakers with a steady crescendo. Louder now. Louder still. Steady. Steady ...*

Somebody hollered, "Brang it, boy!"

"Brang it on home!"

"We's needin' it 'bout now!"

Wolf pursed his lips and from somewhere deep in the center of the earth, a thousand coyotes howled.

The reverb from the PA buzzed, squealed, popped, and craaaackled ...

"Whoooahh I axed her fo' watuh'/ Whoooahh an' she brought me gasoline/ dat's duh terriblest woman-ooooo/ dat I evuh seeeeeeeen!"

The whole room swayed one-and-two-and-three-and-four-and Wolf howled. Everybody howled.

"Sang da song, chile! Sang it!" they yelled.

"Whoooahh da chu'ch bell tonin'/ Whoooahh da hearse gone drivin' slow/ I hope my babeeeee/ Don' leave me no mooooohh'!"

This moment ... Don't never forget it ...

PART ONE

MIDNIGHT CREEPIN'

It was enough to make yo' son, mama, wish he's dead and gone.
—ROBERT WILKINS

WHEN I'M UPSET, BLOOD LEAKS FROM MY HEAD. That's the truth —I'm not trying to bullshit you. I don't know if you folks even use "bullshit" as a verb. At all. Oh well. When I'm over the edge, my gums bust open and my nose bleeds and the whites of my eyes get little red polka dots on them. I only mention that because my eyes really hurt right now. They probably look like crimson marbles with black holes in the middle. It's been a stressful couple of days. I've been hiding out in these woods since I got here. I stole this paper and these pencils from a schoolhouse two miles that way. I wish there had been paints instead. Don't really write normally. Just writing this to keep from going totally Bellevue. I don't even know if anyone will ever read this.

My name is Eli Cooper. I'm a twenty-seven year old "neo-post-impressionist," or so I'm told. *If Edvard Munch and Jackson Pollock had a child* and so on. Anyway, I am—was—the toast of the Village back home. I had the freshest agent, the dopest shows in the choicest galleries, the flyest reviews ... I could clean my brushes on an old T-shirt and the *Voice* would call it "The boldest statement in art since *Piss Christ*." I had the smartest friends. I had the prettiest wife—

My nose is bleeding.

So you're probably wondering what NYC's flashiest flash-in-the-pan of the new millennium is doing stranded in the backwoods of Mississippi in 1938. So am I. So am I. So am I. So am I.

There goes my nose again.

❋

6   Nathan Singer

DONTPANIC
✳

BACK HOME I had just been hired to do a jacket piece for this noise punk outfit, The Sleepy October. I hate them. I hate that whole bullshit scene. No-talent fucks.

"We're all about shifting into a new punk paradigm," their junkie slut lead singer told me. Horrid. HORRID!

But my agent Marcus pushed it on me.

"We can reach the *teen market*, Eli!" he'd say. "Like street cred with bigger payoff." Like that means something to me. I'm a tortured artist or whatever. I've got a reputation to think about.

I only took the whore job because Jessie wanted a bigger apartment. Jessie's my wife. Jessie Davis-Cooper. My mahogany queen. My little bitty pretty one. She's a dancer with an African drum and dance troupe. "Neo-tribalist." Everybody's "neo" in NYC. Go figure.

"You should grab this opportunity," she'd say. "You'd be a crazy not to. We can have a whole new life. We deserve it, Li-la."
Li-la. Miss that already.

So yeah, I detest the New York noise scene. I love the old stuff (well ... I guess it's not old to you). Big Mama Thornton. Duke Ellington. Billie Holiday. Son House ... Howlin' Wolf. (Howlin' Wolf. Something weird about Howlin' Wolf ...) I'd put on some scratchy old jazz or blues compilation LP and Jess would laugh at me.

But after a refrain or two, hell yeah, she'd start to dance. God. Her dancing ... like no one else ...
Wish I could see her now.

✽

GODDAMN BOILING fucking hot here. Covered in a layer of slime and grit. The air is not even humid. It's solid. Like breathing casserole. Try to sleep. Sleep it off. Sleep it away. Maybe wake up somewhere else. Good night, Jessie. I'm sorry I didn't get a chance to say good-bye.

"THE EMPEROR'S FUCKING NAKED, BABY!" *That's what I told her.* "The emperor is fucking naked."

"Li-la, don't be such a dramatic. Do this cover art, and—"

"—And what? Burn in "Sell-out Hell" for all eternity?"

"You call it "Sell-out Hell," I call it a phat Soho co-op and no worries. Tomato, tomahto."

"Jess, have you *heard* this music?"

"Oh, let me guess. It doesn't sound like Bessie Smith or Robert Nighthawk or Skip James and they don't record in mono into a tin horn. Right? I swear, Li-la, you are an old man trapped in a young man's body. No, scratch that. You are an old BLACK man trapped in a white boy's body."

"Marcus is just trying to turn me into the next—"

"Marcus is a good agent and he wants what's best for you and you know it. I'm asking you, please, just this once. Take this one *whore job* and I'll never ask for anything ever again. You'd be a crazy not to grab this opportunity."

"'Crazy' is an adjective, sweetheart. Not a noun." She always did that. No idea why.

"It could be the start of something great. This could be your chance. We could have a whole new life."

"I know."

I know.

"We deserve it."

"It's just ... shallow."

"What is?"

"All this stuff. Meaningless. Hipper-than-thou drivel. Fake plastic hash. Gives you cancer of the spirit. I hate it."

"You hate everything. You want to leave New York?"

"I didn't say that."

"Where would be 'deep' enough for you, Mr. Neo-post-impressionism?"

Deep enough for me. Where would be deep enough for me ...

"You're my angel, Jessie. My little bitty pretty one."

"You're my little school boy. Inlovewitchoo, Li-la Delila."

Inlovewitchoo too.

❈

THE NIGHT I WAS WORKING on the album art for those Warhol-loving twats The Sleepy October, Jessie had a gig down at the Burroughs Theater. Two weeks past my deadline, you know? She understood.

"I should be there. It's opening night."

"There will be plenty of other shows. There will be plenty of other opening nights, Mr. Takin'-My-Time."

The piece was turning out pretty decent. Sort of Baconesque, but not *overtly* derivative. (Anybody who can accept a concept like "neo-post-impressionism" should be able to accept any bucketful of dog snot splattered on a canvas.) I fell asleep on my tarp sometime after midnight. I was awakened all covered in paint by the sound of the phone ringing and my friend Serj screaming on the answering machine—

"Li?! Oh shit Li! You gotta get down to St. Luke's!!! It's Jess! There's been a terrible—"

I grabbed the first cab that stopped and busted ass to the hospital.

But I—

was too late.

always too late hours too late I was two hours too always too late

Backstage at the Burroughs Theater, a riser had fallen on Jess and broken her spine.

My baby's dead.

My baby girl's dead.

My little bitty pretty …

I don't fucking feel like writing anymore

❋

THEY COULDA KEPT THE WHOLE GODDAMN THING the whole fucking piece of shit goddamn art crowd nonsense didn't mean a goddamn anything ... I'd do anything ... never needed to be an artist wasn't a calling it was a skill a trade like jack hammering or something I'd work a day shift at Dunkin Donuts + a night shift dishing out blowjobs at the Manhole in Chicago to HAVE HER BACK!!!!!!!!!!!!!!!!!!!!!!!!!!!!!!!!!!!

please goddamn it

PLEASE ANYTHING

please anything

✻

WHY

WHY

WHY

WHY

WHY

WHY

WHY

WHY

WHY

WHY

WHY

WHY

WHY

WHY

WHY

WHY

WHY

WHY

WHY

WHY

WHY

❋

WHY?!
!
!
!
!
!
!
!
!
!
!
!
!
!
!
!
!
!
!
!
!
!
!
❋

OKAY.

Calmer now.

When I finally got to the hospital … they said she never felt a thing because she never woke up. I started spitting and screaming like—

I was possessed. I tried to strangle myself with my dreadlocks and I tried to bash my head into a wall but Serj and Amie and these two big orderlies grabbed onto me and I finally wriggled free and went screaming out into the streets.

I was hoping a car would hit me.

No luck.

I ran in whatever direction my boots would lead me.

Somebody fucking kill me.

I finally fell over and passed out in the grass. I thought I was in Central Park.

Don't know if I was or not.

When I woke up, it looked like I was right smack dab in the middle of Monet's *Poppy Fields*. I wandered into the woods and found a noose hanging from a tree branch. I tried reaching for it.

Too weak.

Gave up.

I slammed my left temple into the tree trunk, but that only made me nauseous.

As I sat there crying like a damn infant, this little kid wanders up to me. Little Black kid in brown rags that looked at least two sizes too small for him. I said "Hi" and he ran off screaming about a monster a monster.

I probably do look like some sort of Medusa-creature with these long knots hanging off my head. And the piercings and all. Well, figuring somebody with a shotgun would probably be following the kid back, I took off. Don't know why. So eager to end it all just minutes before. Go figure.

Night after night I would sneak around trying to find a decent place to sleep and figure out where the fuck I was. During that thunderstorm a couple of nights ago, after completely freaking out some horses sleeping in a barn up by the creek, I found the school-house where I got these pencils and whatnot. Under the teacher's desk was a newspaper. *Clarion-Ledger*.

Under the header, it read:

Thursday, July 7, 1938.

That's how I found myself here with you good people.

I don't understand it either.

So what do I do now?

> My grandparents are teenagers.
> I think I'll go hunt them down and kill them.
> Just to see what happens.

I KNOW IF ANY OF YOU FIND THESE PAGES, you'll hunt *me* down and string me up. Or put me in the "nervous hospital." Fine with me. But you're gonna have to catch me first.

❋

HOW

DID

THIS

HAPPEN

?

❋

KEEP HAVING WEIRD FLASHES OF THAT NIGHT. *That night.*

Fell asleep on the tarp. In the paint. Tripped when I heard Serj on the machine.

GOTTAWAKEUPNOW!

Tripped again running down the stairs. Cabs won't stop.

STOP MOTHERFUCKERS!

I was two hours too always too late.

GODDAMN THIS!

It will never never never never go away!! I'm fucking trapped in it!!!!!!!

This one moment. I'm trapped forever in this moment.

oh god gotta get it together gotta gotta get it get it—

❀

ALL RIGHT NOW. I. Am. Adequately. Chilled. Out.

When I finally got a cab to pick me up, this bag lady walked right in front of the car and stopped and stood there. Just stopped and stared at our brownstone. She was carrying boards or canvas or some shit and I'm screaming at the cabbie and he's screaming at the lady—

"Move yer black ass, heifer!"

DRIVE YOU BASTARD DRIVE!!!

White—bonnet—thing.

She was wearing some white and brown smock lookin' dress and a little white head-wrap bonnet lookin' deal.

She ran off and this bearded guy starts spraying and wiping the windshield.

The bearded guy had on a green slicker.

Of all the things to remember.

I tripped on the stairs at the hospital too.

Never even got the chance to say good-bye.

MISSISSIPPI. Center of the universe.

JULY 10, 1938

May as well make this a journal. Nobody will ever read this shit anyway. I appear to be just on the outskirts of West Point, Mississippi. Right outside of the "downtown" area which sure as hell doesn't look like much. B and E is getting to be second nature. There are no alarms on anything and I don't take enough to arouse suspicion. Some soap here, some shoes there. A shirt here, the pants somewhere else. Little bits of money at every stop. Last night I stole a suitcase. Also made off with a state map. Looks like ferries run out of Natchez. Could be useful. How many goddamn towns are in this state? I'll probably get rid of the map. Can't read it too well anyway. Gotta try and find a national map. See what's north.

I've made the decision to try and make my way during the daylight when there are folks around. Blend in. Assimilate. When I get my moxie up, of course. I stole a razor and some scissors from Woolworth's and I've been cleaning up in their back room after hours. I took out all my earrings, my eyebrow rings, my nose chain, my nipple rings, and the barbell in my tongue. I also cut all my dreads off. Shaved clean. Figure by the time my hair grows back, I'll be ready to face the world. Without giving myself away, I've been trying to watch people. Absorb their mannerisms. Study their habits like I'm Jane fuckin' Goodall.
I feel like Frankenstein's creature.

JULY 11, 1938

One time I told Marcus that I wanted to get out of NY for a while.

"But babe!" he said, "Your work doesn't play in LA! They're not ready for it yet." I told him I didn't want to go to LA either, so he says, "What, you wanna go to Mars? Eli, there is no world outside LA and New Yawk."

My hair is starting to fuzz out a little. I still look like somebody's dick.

JULY 13, 1938

I keep waking up at night. Feeling like somebody's watching. Like somebody's walking behind me. Nobody's there, goddamn it.

I drew a picture of Jess today. Nice to see I can still do realism. Tore the fucker up.

Last night I broke into Connor Hardware & Supply and ganked a book of drafting paper and a set of watercolors. Hell yeah.

Just had a weird memory! "The Restaurant and Social Club for Explorers and Mad Scientists." I can't believe this just dawned on me. I was hanging out, of all places, at The Jekyll and Hyde Club about a month before that night. (1409 Avenue of the Americas NYC ... I just wanted to remember.) I'd gotten so burned on the too-cool-for-school boho scene pits that I had come to much prefer gimmicky tourist joints like J & H. Even that was getting a little too precious for me. Next stop: Applebee's. But that night, yeah, that was a good night for being bothered when I'm trying to work. No sooner had I sat down then these two skaterpunk kids from Cincinnati, Ohio or some such place come up to me all excited. They'd seen a feature on Jess and me in Asylum Press and were talking a mile a minute about ... well, I don't really know ... art and dance and music and whatnot (big fans of The Sleepy October, apparently). I told them that Jessie had a performance that weekend and if they gave me their names I'd get them on the guest list (which I did, thank you very much). That sent them on their way happy as little clams.

So then I'm just sitting there on my own, working out some new ideas, just sketching stuff at random. I'm kind of just penciling out these three cats sitting at a corner booth dressed to the nines—Armani suits, the whole deal—when across the room I see this *man*. Huge, barrel-chested black man, maybe a year or two older than I am, wearing a brown derby and a string tie. Looked totally out of place. For real. Although I can't possibly imagine where this fellow would have fit in. Couldn't help but think that I recognized him from somewhere, but I could not for the life of me place where. Not too long after I notice him, he looks directly at me and gives me this smile—a friendly, but kinda sinister sort of smile. He walks over and sits at my table.

"What ah yuh drinkin', suh?" he asks in this deep, husky southern drawl.

"Gin and tonic," I say.

So he orders us two doubles. *Where do I know this guy from?* His voice made him even more familiar, but I still couldn't place it.

"Di'n't we meet some tahme ago in Belzonia?"

"Where is that?"

"Mississippi."

"I've never been to Mississippi." *I've never been to Mississippi ... I've never been to Mississippi!*

"Mah mistake," he shrugged. "Good to meet ya now anyways. Mah frens call meh Chess. And you's Eli Cooper?"

"That's me."

"Kinda famous, eh?" He laughed, pointing at the two kids.

"Gettin' there."

He said he'd seen me around. With Jessie.

"Now that there's one pretty lady. You's a sho' 'nuff lucky man."

Weird. He was a really nice guy, though. Chess. We talked for about twenty minutes about this and that. I did anyway. He didn't really say too much except, right before leaving he asks me, "So which is you, Missah Coopah? If'n this is a restr'nt an' social club fo' explorers an' mad scientists, which is you?"

Then he laughs this bellowing laugh, shakes my hand (about broke it) ... and notices the sketch of the three Armani suits at the bar. Tenses up tight, like a fist. He looks over at them and they smile at us ... real ... sickly kinda.

"Goddamn," Chess whispered. "You gots to be careful, hear?"

And he was gone.

Told Jessie about it later and she just shrugged.

"Psycho fans. Your art sure brings out the peculiars."

Maybe Jekyll and Hyde has something to do with all this! The joint was established in 1931, seven years ago. So it's there right now! If I can get to New York, maybe I can get some answers. If nothing else, I'll be in a familiar place. What do I have to lose?

✳

JULY 16, 1938

In exactly one month Robert Johnson, the king of the Delta blues, will die. Down in the Delta outside Greenwood, Johnson will drink from a poisoned bottle of whiskey at a jukejoint—Three Forks. It's a trippy feeling, knowing what's gonna happen. I'm thinking about taking a trip down to Three Forks to watch it. The presence of a mysterious white man at Robert Johnson's fatal final performance will most certainly alter the mythology for all time. How cool is that!

I will dick up the future if I damn well feel like it. Fuck Ray Bradbury.

I know I'm probably gonna look back and kick my own ass for writing this, but once that hellacious sun goes down and you get used to the crickets, it's actually kinda beautiful out here. It's really quiet and the air is clean ... THICK, *heavy*, but clean. And there are about four gazillion stars. That's an approximation, of course.

It is incredibly hot, though. And those little black bugs, gnats I guess, they get caked in the corners of your eyes. You wipe and wipe and wipe and there's always this film of dead black gunk right in your peripheral vision. Oh well. I give up.

The watercolors are working out great. I've been doing a lot of landscapes. Should have been doing landscapes all along. I'm a natural.

Have hair again. Tomorrow morning I'm gonna go into town. Just gotta remember to be polite, act natural, speak slowly, and double all syllables.

Robert Johnson lost his wife too. Giving birth. Killed her and their baby. Some people say that incident is what made Johnson curse the name of God and clinch the decision to sell his soul. After August 16th, there will be black folks all over this state saying, "Robert Johnson is burning in Hell." If you ask me, I'd say homeboy got fucked over with the 1-2 punch.

Sketched another Jess picture. I'm keeping this one.

❊

July 17, 1938

Well I was nervous as hell at first, but everything is going okay. Asked the guy at Connor's Hardware (yeah I went in there—how's that for big brass balls!) where I might find some work. I told him I just got out of the Navy (thus the tattoos) and came through on a Natchez ferry by way of New Orleans. *Man. I hope I got that right.* He seemed to buy it.

"Now lemme git this straight, son," he whistled through his teeth, "Yew jus'n came from N'Orl'ins tuh West Point, Mississippi lookin' fer work. Ain' nobody tole ya? Ther ain't no work here no how. Les'n you's a nigger, huh huh. Yew ain't a nigger, son, huh huh."

Well, obviously I didn't want to stand around talking to this asshole all day, so away I went. Some folks have been staring at me, I guess 'cause I'm new, but I've found that a smile, a wave, and a *Good Morning*! will win them right over. I did that in New York one time and a guy pissed on my duffle bag.

❉

July 20, 1938

Three days. Goddamn.

But I think my luck has changed for the better. I met a really cool guy in this joint called Charlie's Place. His name is Lennis. Lennis Martin I think. Quite a friendly gent once he decided not to pound me into a fine paste.

It was shaping up to be just as fruitless a day as the past few had been. Hot and tired and seriously stressing out, I'm sitting at this Charlie's Place drinking a soda. Yeah, I was in there a while because I had no where else to go, obviously. And I am the only customer. The only one. I heard some chattering in the back room and I could tell they were talking about me. You know, you can just tell. Well, this big, red-haired guy comes in after a while hollering good afternoons to everybody and before too long his friend from the back room (who I found out was named Joe and runs the place) is all whispering to him and pointing at me. *Fuck.*
So you know he's just got to come around and park himself right at my table.

"Sir, I don't believe I've seen you around. Are ya new?"
Here we go …

"That's right," I said. "I've been seeking gainful employment and some manner of safe lodging, but it hasn't been going well."

"You don't say. Ha ha. Well, that certainly is an original idea. Most folks looking for work *leave* Mississippi. They don't come here. Ha ha ha! Now, we don't want to appear inhospitable, but Joe tells me you've been sittin' here most of the afternoon nursin' on a Cherry Coke. Says you had a spot of blood on your face earlier. Ya hurt?"

"No. When I get … No, I'm not hurt."

"Then maybe you'd better go on and take your business elsewhere, friend."
Bwoy, yew ain' frum rond heah', is ye?

"I don't see why I should have to leave if I'm not causing any trouble. This dump doesn't have any customers anyway. Friend."

Yep, that did it.

"Now you look-a-here," he said, darkening. "Joe is a close personal friend of mine and I'm not having strangers come into his place ... " and on and on and on.

Could I have just kept my trap shut? Could I have just nodded and sulked away muttering under my breath? Could have. But nah ...

"Listen, Jerk-ass. I'm just sitting here minding my own. If you have beef with me, then—"

And he immediately stands up. *Fuuuuck.* Towering over me. So I get up, defiant, tough guy face on (and quaking in my friggin' boots). We're all squared off and shit. Lennis has his hands balled into fists (looked like rocks wrapped in tanned leather). And we're standing there and neither one of us is moving. So I'm like, IT'S ON! I grab this fork off the table, and I'm gonna jab him good, but it slips out of my hand, so I dive onto the floor to get it and I stab myself in the wrist with it, which hurt like hell, but I'm up and I LUNGE across the table, fork in hand, aimed right for this dude's gut, but see ... I didn't factor the actual length of the table, which was slightly too long ... and I'm just stabbing at the air. And he's just looking at me. Blank.

Total disbelief.

Not even stepping back or nothing.

But I'm not giving up! I'm gonna run him through with this damn fork!!! Jab jab jab!

At nothin'.

And finally ... He just pulled it outta my hand. *I'm done.*

Of all the various ways I ever thought I might die, getting beat to death in a greasy spoon in West Point, Mississippi during the Great Depression wasn't even on the list. But there I was, splayed across the table, waiting for the blows to commence ... and he starts laughing.

"What in blazes did you plan to do with this!"

I mean laughing *hard*. Saying something about "tarnations" and whatnot, I can't really make it out. So I'm pretty much humiliated and I mumbled some idiocy about the fork being the great equalizer ... and then we both fell out laughing. He bought me another Coke and we ended up shooting the breeze for quite a while. And hey hey! He invited me back to his house for supper, and here I am.

His wife Anna made us chicken and corn muffins and some brown stuff that kinda tastes like salty oatmeal. It was good as hell whatever it was. Anna's really pleased with my big appetite (yeah, I've been eating berries and stolen buttermilk since I got here). I think I handled myself with her questions fairly well, and kept the lying to a minimum.

"So, Eli. Navy brought you to West Point. What are your plans now?"

"Well, my dream always was to paint. I love art. But I suppose that's not going to put any food on my table … or even *get* me a table. So you know … "

"Oh now don't give up the dream. Ya ain't married, are ya?"
Shit. Be cool about this.

"To tell … the honest truth, ma'am, I'm a widower. Been years now, you understand, but it still feels like just a few days … "

"I'm so sorry, Eli."

"It's okay."
It's okay.

"You poor—"

"No, it's all right. I'm learning. I'm growing. She was a dancer. In New York. Actually almost famous. Kinda. Getting there, you know? It was an accident back stage one night. A riser propped against the wall slipped and … they said she never felt a thing because she never woke up."

"And so young too … "

"Yes ma'am."
And so young, too …

"I don't know what I'd do if I ever lost this one here," she said nodding toward Lennis.

"I'll tell ya what she'd do," Lennis said winking at me, "Spend all her time beatin' away all the local—"

"OH, YOU GET OUTTA HERE!" Anna wailed, punching Lennis in the shoulder, her face ruby red. We laughed like hell.

They're AWESOME.

Lennis says he works on a farm about four miles out of town. As luck (?) would have it, they need a new guy since one of the crew got his fingers pulled off in a hay baling accident. Lennis says the pay is pretty low, but it's probably the best thing going. Also, there's a boarding house run by an older lady named Durning. She'll put me up cheap and it's pretty close to the farm.

I told Lennis and his wife that Eli is a biblical name. I don't know if it is or not.

Changed my mind about the Robert Johnson thing.

JULY 21, 1938
"quittin' time"

God, this is the worst job anyone has ever had to do. The farm is a fucking plantation—at least I guess it is, knowing what I know about plantations. It's about seven thousand degrees in the shade out here. Lift! Toss! Stack! Lift toss stack. Lift toss stack. For twelve straight goddamn hours. I threw up after six. Thankfully nobody saw me. There is a crew of Black folks working on the lower half of the field. We are on the upper portion. Lots of, "Nigra this, nigra that." To his credit, Lennis didn't really hang with that. He's not a real talkative kind of guy most of the time. The shit I've been telling him has got to sound completely wacko. (Like my "Navy days" and whatnot. What the fuck do I know about the Navy?) But he just nods his head and accepts the whole thing. "Well that's mighty fine," he says. It's good as hell to have somebody to talk to again.

I'm writing this in Lennis's truck. We're riding up to the Durning House. He's looking at me funny 'cause I'm writing so intently. I just told him that I have to write everything down because I'm a "forgitful sumbitch." He laughed.
More later.
Goddamn I'm tired.
✳

JULY 21, 1938
evening

I'm surprised at how nice Mrs. Durning's boarding house is considering how little I'm gonna pay to stay here. She's a sweet old biddy, Mrs. Durning. Just like you'd expect of a fifty-or-so year old southern belle. Little prickly at first, but Lennis is *The Man*.

"Ah don't let *just anyone* passin' through stay hea', Mista Ma'tin. You know that."

"You have my word, ma'am," Lennis said. "He's good folk. And he'll be around awhile. I can vouch for his employment."

"You just met him! Ah am sorreh, but we ahe quite full right now. Ve'y sorreh."

So he whispers to her, real slick, "Mrs. Durning, I wudn't goin' brang this up, on account of I didn't want to embarrass m' friend here. But Mr. Cooper here happens to be one of the *top painters* in New York City."

That got her attention.

"But see," he continued, "He's just here tryin' to get some honest pay, y'understand, what with the hard times and all ... "

"Hmm. Well ... " Mullin' it over, tappin' her shoe.

"See I'm just-a picturin' in my mind your mantle in the parlor and how mighty fine a port—"

"Mista Ma'tin! Certainly you ahe not tryin' to—"

"Oh *no* ma'am. Terrible sorry. No offense intended."

"Still and all ... one must consideh the notion of Christian cha'ity."

"Yer known for nothin' if not godliness, Mrs. Durning."

"And these ahe hahd times."

"Whatsoever you do to the least of my brothers ... " And they both look right at me. *Thanks a lot.*

But it worked! I owe Lennis big time.

"This is a beautiful house, Mrs. Durning," I said as she showed me to my room. And it really is.

"Oh, thank you so much for sayin' so, dea'. Mista Coopah, I hope you'll enjoy y'stay. This used to be Mr. Durning's study befoah he passed away, God rest his soul ... "

There was a sad little moment. Wasn't sure if I should say something ... but soon enough ...

"So! Mista Ma'tin tells me you're an *artiste*."

"Portraits and still-lifes mostly."

"Po'traits you say!" She swooned (I'm not lying ... *swooned*). "Mah stahs, Mista Coopah, I always did want a po'trait of mah own, but well ... " I'm surprised she didn't say "Ah do decla'e." I told her I'd be honored to paint her portrait.

I am so in.

Met one of Mrs. Durning's housekeepers. Girl named Mae, probably late teens/early twenties. Real dark skin—fiiiine little slim (although I probably shouldn't be thinking that in this day and age). Apparently there's another housekeeper too—Ella. I haven't met her yet. I sure heard a lot about her though. She's the apple of Mrs. Durning's eye.

"Po' little Ella, she a widow just lahke me," she said. "James, God rest his soul, died before he could give me a child so my two girls Ella and Mae, they ahe lahke my children. Ella's husband, *tsk tsk* ... well that was just unpleasant, to be certain."

Whatever.

I'm dreading going back to work tomorrow.

❊

JULY 22, 1938

This sheepfuck cracker named Jeb yelled at me today for not oiling the plow. At least I think that's what he said. Where the fuck was that in the job description? After he finished pitching his little bitch fit, I wanted to scream back at him. But I knew better than to get angry, so instead I bugged out my eyes and started shuffle dancing around going, "Yassuh, massa suh. I sho' is sorry sho' nuff." All the other guys laughed their asses off. I'm pretty popular now. I felt kinda bad for doing that, but I have to get in good with these guys. It's just that way sometimes, yeah?

We cut out early today, thank God.
The men on the lower half didn't cut out. And there are children working down there too. Little ones.

Lennis is talking some nonsense about he and Anna taking me to church with them on Sunday. Oh man.

There are four other guys staying at the house besides me (Edmund, Douglas, and I can't remember the other two). Mrs. Durning is flittering around going, "The house is all abuzz again!" You can tell that she's one of those ladies that just really digs having guys around. She told me when I walked in that Ella was outside hanging laundry and I should go out and say "How do" (*I swear to God that's what she said*). I told her that I might in a little while but I needed to scrub up and rest a bit before supper.

"Mah goodness," she said. "Such a hahd workin' young man. Now don't you go hurtin' those talented fingahs of yo's, dea'. That po' man who you replaced, *tsk tsk* ... well that was just unpleasant, to be certain."

Crazy old broad.

Oh God!

✻

OH GOD I DON'T BELIEVE IT!
I just saw "Ella" outside bringing in milk and
goddamn it
God in heaven
I swear to fucking God
almighty

She's Jess!
God help me she's Jess!

PART TWO

DRY LONG SO

The stuff I gots will bust yo' brains out, baby. It'll make you lose yo' mind.
—ROBERT JOHNSON

The Time Walker's Blues ...
or Key to the Highway
by "Jerome Kinnae"

A.

I'll have you know I literally walked through fire to get here.

It's Friday the thirteenth as I write this. 1965. I feel like my skull has been cracked open. I'm in a hideously overcrowded jail, probably Lincoln Heights Jail if I overheard correctly, which is particularly disconcerting because I thought this joint had been closed down. Facilities don't seem to work right, and it is hotter than hellfire. "Hotter'n wild gorilla pussy" as some drunk keeps screaming, and I suppose he'd know.

Some white boy gave me this notebook and pen. He's the only white in here. The only white I've seen in many days in fact, except for cops. And *Them.*

I'm a time walker. That sounds much more dramatic than it actually is. Pretty mundane honestly. It's not actually all that difficult. I realize most people wouldn't even accept that time walking is possible, but it's as commonplace as hang-gliding or suicide. Simple enough to do, but incredibly dangerous. Fatal if you fuck up. And most people do. Time paths are littered with corpses. I'm assuming. I've never seen any bodies on the paths, but they must go *somewhere.*

It's probably Saturday morning by now. Maybe 3AM. My head is pounding. The jail is eerily quiet all of a sudden, which is more than a little unnerving. But after the noise I've lived in for the past two days, I'll take my relief as it comes and deal with consequences as they present themselves.

Before I talk about how I ended up here I would probably be a god-awful bastard if I didn't talk a little about what time walking is. Truth be told, I'm a shade reluctant to do that. Among walkers, writing is considered to be an incredibly foolish and reckless thing to do. Anything that leaves a trail back to you is potential death.

Consider this: have you ever read a true account of time walking until now? There you go.

But to hell with it. I've made a habit of leaving signed, hand-written notes everywhere I land. And sending letters to boot. Why? Sheer arrogance. And recklessness. I admit it. Recklessness is what brings most people to time walking in the first place.

I should confess up front that I'm far from an authority on the subject. I fell into this by accident, and I've just been fortunate enough to get sufficiently old hat at it. I've survived this far; there's the evidence. I don't know with any certainty how or why things work the way they work. So, take what you read here with however much salt you need and understand that these are my personal theories and strictly conjecture on my part. There are many people who are far more skilled and knowledgeable than I, but they would never be so foolhardy as to write about it. So you're stuck with me. If you read this and decide to go out and try it for yourself and you end up torn to pieces or just *gone forever,* it's your own fault.

Very simply put: all over the world there are paths that lead to other times and places. There's nothing magical about it. It's no more fantastic than erosion or stalactites or evolution. It's simply the way the world is constructed. Some paths are easier to navigate than others. Some are impossible and you will die immediately. Some lead many centuries and thousands of miles, some a yard or two and seventeen minutes forward or back.

Knowing where the paths are is elemental to being a success-ful walker. I know twenty-three paths and they are all confined to the United States and the twentieth-century—save two, which currently lead to 2001 (they may shift as time shifts, like mud and water). I've met walkers who know hundreds, if not thousands, of paths that lead to times and places I hope never to go. It's hard enough being a Black man in twentieth-century America.

As I've said there are experienced walkers who know count-less paths and can do things with them beyond the imagination. Most walkers, however, are one-timers. Something, usually some-thing tragic, something devastating, leads them down a path, and wherever they end up they remain. They either choose not to, or are unable to, go back. They manage to convince themselves that where and when they are is where they belong ... or in fact *where they've always been*. And they often live out the rest of their lives gripped in fear and paranoia. *And with good cause.*

To: serjnamie@yahoo.com
From: marc@marcsims.com
Sent: 7/22/01
Subject: guilty

Hey everybody,
You two doing okay? I just wanted to drop a line to see how things
are. I'm getting by over here pretty well all things considered. Did
you see the "This Week In … " in last week's *Asylum Press*? It said
some shit like "The Village community was rocked by tragedy on
July 5 when interpretive dance artist Jessica *David* Cooper was killed
blah blah blah beloved wife of pop artist *Elliot* Cooper bullshit
bullshit missing, *suspected dead*." Well needless to say, I was fucking
pissed and I called and gave that bitch Joel Whatshisname a big slice
of my mind to chew on. He said he would print a correction and an
apology in next week's issue. Whatever.

I was wondering if maybe possibly you guys had heard anything at
all about Eli. I haven't. I'm kind of afraid to. Every time the phone
rings, I'm scared to answer. Keep thinking it's going to be *that call.*
I'm sure you know what I mean.

I feel so fucking guilty about the funeral. I mean, we held off as
long as we could, right?
I was just hoping against hope that he would show up. All day, I
kept looking over my shoulder, but he was never there.

The thing is I could have sworn he *was* there! I could have sworn
I saw him. In my peripheral vision, you know? But I'd look, and
he wouldn't be there. That's how you felt too, right Amie? Isn't
that what you said? I think we all need some serious couch time. I
know I do. Thought I saw Jessie the other day too. Sweartochrist.
That's the red flag—you see your deceased friend walking around
in downtown traffic, it's time for a shrink sesh.
Sorry, guys. I'm just purging I guess.

Well anyway, I gotta go. I got clients to represent and all that. Speaking of which:

Serj, hit me on my cell or drop an e-mail as soon as you can. I still want to have your show on August 6. I hope you're gonna be ready by then. We gotta stay focused. Jessie would want us to. And I just know that Eli is gonna pop up real soon and we can all get back to our lives.

And we'll be a family again.

I love you guys.

Marcus

To: marc@marcsims.com
From: serjnamie@yahoo.com
Sent: 7/22/01
Subject: RE: guilty

Hey-ho, Marcus.

Well, the waterworks are still running hard over here. I can't stop crying. Serj hasn't left the studio since the funeral. He's almost got *Eyes Over Jess* finished. It's Beautiful. Beautiful with a capital B. He's talking about doing a companion piece for it (know what I mean?), but I don't think that's a good idea. No need to worry. He'll definitely be ready by the 6th.

I agree with you. Everybody needs some major downtime. Just like I told you, I keep seeing things that aren't there. Chill out, I'm not hallucinating.

It's just little … things. Here and there. Just—you know … Okay. So I need medication. Life goes on. LOL.

I'm trying to make sense of it all. Trying to find a meaning, y'know? I really really wish there was somebody or something, you know, keeping it all together. Keeping time and space in check, and all that bullshit …

Now I know what you're thinking, Marc, and no, I'm not gonna get religious on you.

Peep this: Yesterday, I wanted to give Serj some Serj-time, so I went for a walk in Central, and I'm feeling super down. Super way down. There I am just walking and bumming, and there's this little boy, maybe seven or eight, sitting in the grass. Just sitting and drawing, right? Sweetest little thing, I wanted to squeeze him to pieces. He sees me, gets up, and walks over.

"You ought not be so blue, ma'am," he said in the cutest Southern accent, "Here y' go."

And he gave me a sketch of a tree with flowers blooming on it. It was really good work! There was a little face in the corner soooooooooooooo cute.

I said thank you very much, and he nodded and turned to walk away. "I best to get on," he said, "Granddad get cross if I stay 'way too long. You can have this one too. It ain't mine."

He handed me this odd pencil drawing of a dirt road. I'd know this style anywhere, Marc! I'd know it anywhere. In the corner, in the bottom right corner, it said: Li81438.

"Whose picture is this?" I said, turning to see the boy. But he was gone. Totally vanished.

I'll show you the sketch when I see you again. I'm sure it's just some bullshit bootleg or something. Everybody and their uncle is biting off Eli's style right now. It's damn close, though. Looks like the shit he did in college. Maybe you know what these numbers mean? C—ya soon, keep your head up, have some coke and a smile. We'll all be a-okay.

Love back atcha,
Amie

JULY 22, 1938

It's late as hell now. I can't sleep. Think I'm gonna be sick.

Tried to play it cool at dinner. Don't even recall what we ate. "Ella," whoever the fuck she is, didn't react to me at all. Just a big, rehearsed smile and a "Nahce to meet you, Missah Coopah." Served the food, smiled, and bowed.

All I could do was keep my head down and try to keep calm. What else could I do? What can I do? *What can I do?* Damn nosebleed. Gotta lay on my back.

This has all gotta mean something, right? Why would I be here and why would she—
Are we supposed to be—

Like this?

It doesn't seem right at all. Not at all. How?

If we're supposed to be together here in this godforsaken mudpit town, in this godforsaken decade, then ... I don't know. Why doesn't she know me? *Why doesn't she know me?!* Is this some sort of big cosmic joke? Why?
Is this Mississippi or Hell?
There's gotta be somebody who can tell me what's going on.

❋

GOOD MORNING LADIES!

And it is a simply delightful day today. I am off to my Saturday bridge game with Mrs. Grant and the rest, but I will be back later on in the afternoon. We need fresh fish and vegetables, so if one of you could run to the Piggly Wiggly today, that would be fine indeed.

Mae, don't forget to hang the linen. We must take advantage of that sunshine! Ella, I would like you to go to Ralph Cole's furniture shop down on Handlesfield and pick up a few record albums to play on the Victrola. If we are going to have guests in the house, we should entertain them. And they surely won't want me to sing! You can pick up a record for yourself and Mae if you like, so long as it is clean and proper and you don't pester the guests with it.

One last thing while it is still on my mind, I think Mister Cooper up in James's old study is feeling ill. I'm sure you all saw how poorly he looked at supper last night and he did not go in to work today. He hasn't left his room. If one of you could bring him up some soup and tea, that would be fine. Have a good day now!

Sincerely,
Mrs. Durning

JULY 23, 1938

Well, I suppose I'm gonna have to go to work on Monday, or else move back into the woods. But I'm not leaving this room until then. No meals, no goddamn church, nothing. And no more writing. Ever. Just painting. I have a couple of sheets of paper left and I'll go get a sketch book on Monday. I'm just gonna paint paint paint *paint paint* until my fucking fingers break.

Back in the day some people thought my work was too dark. Shit. They hadn't seen anything.

Somebody's knocking. I'll wait 'til they go away before I open the door.

Damn it Jessie

how could you be—

no more writing

DEAR DIARY,

It is Saturday July the 23rd in the year of Our Lord 1938.

Taking my afternoon break and I surely deserve it. Been a running round madwoman all day. Mae done let the linens to fly all over the grass on account of her not fastening the pins correct on the line. That fool girl going be the death of me. She wanting me to sneak out with her tonight and go to Caledonia to see Big Foot Chester—or Bull Cow or Howlin' Wolf or whatever he's callin hisself these days. I said no Mae I will not be going there. That man scares me badly. He ain't like a natural man. It's like he got the devil in him or something awful. Mae says Ella, you just bein silly. That child calling me silly. Well any old way, to cheer her up, I pick up a record album that she likely to enjoy. Mrs. Durning sent me to fetch a few records for the guests to play on the phonograph. Said I could get something clean and proper for Mae and me to listen to. Well, I done bought us Memphis Minnie singing Dirty Mother For You which ain't rightly clean and proper at all so don't tell nobody Diary shhhhhhh. Our secret.

Wanting to play this here record before Mrs. D come home and the mens get home from work but I can't on account of a Mr. Eli Cooper who shut hisself up in the study all day. He ain't left for nothing. Not when his friend Mr. Martin come over, not even when Mae brung him up some vegetable soup. I should play the record anyway but I reckon he probably don't much like blues music.

I believe I will play it anyway. If he come out to complain at least we know he ain't dead.

His eyes was red as apples at supper last night. That is surely cause Mae don't dust like a house should be dusted proper (Lordy! I picking on Mae today!).

Most likely shouldn't be thinking nothing of this, but I been bothered since that Mr. Eli Cooper come here. There something frightful bout him. I can't reason it for certain, but the second I seen him I thought that I already done knew him. I swear to the Good Lord Above!

My first mind was to run up and throw my arms round him! Now what brung that on? Praise Jesus I minded myself and just bowed a friendly hello. He seem so nervous round me I don't rightly know how to be. Maybe he don't like colored women none. He is a sure enough peculiar. A sure enough peculiar alright.

Well, that will do for the time being, Diary. Gotta put on Memphis Minnie now or we might never get to hear her.

God bless Mae, and Mrs. D, and our guests, and Charlie and Alberta in Alabama, and also God bless Mama and Daddy and Mr. James and my loving Walter up in Heaven.

JULY 23, 1938

I know I said I wasn't gonna write anymore but I had to get this last thing down just in case I'm going completely insane. I think I hear one of my favorite songs playing downstairs.

It's Memphis Minnie—"Dirty Mother For You!!!"

Dear Eli,

Lennis told me that you was poorly today so I fix you up a little something I give to folks who aint feeling right. Careful! Its spicy! I hope your not to sick to go to church with us tomarrow like we talked on. Remember you are always welcome to stay with us if things aint going right for you. Well I hope you feel better soon. Make sure you get plenty of sleep now and drink lots of water. Lennis will be by to pick you up in the morning. Please dont forget to bring me the bowl back when you are done. Its my best bowl. Take care and God bless.

Yours in Christ
Anna Martin

DEAR DIARY,

It is still Saturday July the 23rd in the year of Our Lord 1938.

Mae still giving me grief bout this sneakin out business. She trying to wear me down so I give in. Ella, she say, it ain't but a short ways to Caledonia, and we both grown womens and Mrs. D can't tell us how to be when we done finished working. She got a good point, but I just don't feel like I should be putting my situation at risk. Ain't much else work for me out there. I ain't goin to Caledonia tonight. Mae can just go on by herself for goodness sake. It being so short a ways and all.

A really strange happened bout an hour ago. Me and Mae was straightening up the parlor listening to Memphis Minnie—who by the by, Diary, ain't from Memphis at all. She from Walls Mississippi. Mississippi the center of it all. Any old way, me and Mae, we was dancing with our brooms and laughing and just clowning when who should come creeping down the stairs looking like he done rose from the dead, but that Mr. Eli from the study room. Mae and me, we trying to pretend like we was hard at working but it was too late for that. Mr. Eli, he come in and say That is a great song, one of my favorites. So I says that, Yes I really like it but it is a mite dirty. Mae, the princess of nonsense, she rolling her eyes, shaking her head. Then Mr. Eli starts to saying really odd things like, I use to listen to that song years ago when I was in the Navy. Years and years ago. So many years ago.

But Diary, that song only three years old! I think he must have a fever. Something ain't right with the man. Well I done told you he was a peculiar. Reckon he set Mae to be on edge cause she excused herself to go to Piggly Wiggly.

So Mr. Eli and me, we was scrambling for things to talk about then. I ask him if he was still going to paint a picture of Mrs. Durning and he said that he reckoned he would. Then, all nervous like, he ask me if it was all right if he make MY picture some time. Well I told him if that is what he wanted to do that it would be fine. That made him to light up some. And it made me glad too, Diary. It really truly did and I can't reason what for.

Well shortly after he excused hisself to go back to his room on account of he had to get over his cold so he could go to church tomorrow with the Martins, and I said that reminds me. I went and
fetched him the letter and the bowl of stew that Mrs. Anna Martin
drop off for him. And then he say—

I don't know why I got to be writing all this nonsense. Don't even
know this man. It is just what I been thinking on. Got to go now
Diary.
God bless everybody I already done mentioned earlier.

B.

I am of the belief that *police* are a naturally occurring phenomenon. Just as certain members of a school of fish or collective of amphibians will change gender to suit the needs of the community, or how homosexuality and asexuality increase as populations get too large, police simply *happen* in order to maintain order. All "regular" societies have their police. Time walkers have *Them*.

It seems that every walker has his own name for *Them*. The Pigs, The Dogs, The Slicks, Hell Hounds, Coyotes, The Dancers (I don't fully understand that one), The Swells, Snakes, Devils, Crows, Vultures, Demons, Spooks, Pin-Stripes, and my personal favorite, Irvine. (Some of these are very time-and-geo specific. Irvine is the slang term given to white cops in Southern California during the sixties, which is where I am now. That term somehow got used to refer to *Them* by walkers from here. And I get worried whenever I hear a walker refer to *Them* as Pin-Stripes. Leads me to assume that their knowledge is confined to a particular path that leads from Central Park in Manhattan circa early twenty-first century to West Point, Mississippi, Depression era. The Pin-Stripes, also known as Hell Hounds in that area, are furious right then. And *They* are on a rampage. Unfortunate, because I left some very important cargo there. That is my favorite path and one that I am eager to get back to as soon as I get out of here … but it is *deadly*.)

❋

DEAR DIARY,

Oh goodness! I just had to write this down now to be sure I don't forget. It is late, very late, and Mae and me just snuck in. That girl done talked me into going with her to Caledonia tonight. Now I know that I said I weren't going to do that, but I went and did anyhow. Lordy, it all seem a swirl in my head. I got to remember just right on account of I don't rightly know what really happen.

Mae and me, once we done all our cleaning up for the evening, went off to retire to our room like usual. We says good night to Mrs. Durning and everything just fine. Then we go tipping our toes on down to the road all sneaky like as if we was runaway slaves. Down there a young field hand Negro in his Sunday finest waiting for us with a Terraplane! Mae done met him at the Piggly Wiggly and honey talked him into driving us. Evening ladies, he say, I sure is excited to see the Wolf tonight for I got a notion he going be right magic. Right magic indeed.

Well, Mae she kissing on this man the whole way, giggling and carrying on like a fool. We get to Crawdaddy's jookhouse and, Diary, all I could think on is what Mrs. D always saying. She say Those places ain't fit for a proper lady of any color. Well I hate to say but she may be right. Folks is drinking and swearing and fighting like they ain't goodly Christians. We go in and the Mississippi Sheiks is playing. Now I like the way they sounding so I got to dancing right away. Some mens was watching me like they got a mind to get fresh, but word got round quick that this here Walter Brown's widow so they kept a respectful distance. Mae she left that poor field hand soon as she got a glass of whisky in her and, well, soon as Howlin' Wolf took stage. There weren't no introducing. Nothing. Just all of the sudden that huge beast of a man he crawl up on stage on all fours with all the powers of Hades in his eyes! He growling and snapping and he grab that microphone and I swear to the Good Lord above the windows got to shaking from the noise that man made with his throat! Mae she grabbing for him saying, Chester I loves you! and she weren't the only foolish there that night. I gots to admit though, I was sure overtook. He sang for bout an hour—some the deepest blues this country girl ever did hear. But this where it get so odd.

After Wolf done spent hisself, hollering and flinging his big self to the stage and blowing his harp like he gots a mind to kill it, he walk off stage and come right for me. Right for me!

Womens left and right they start to pouting cause he ain't paying them no mind and writing down suchandso on little sheets of paper and putting them in his guitar case, but he just come right up to me and he say, I been hopin you was comin Miss Jessie. You gots to tell him come find me.

Now what on God's good earth could that be? I says to him, I sure sorry Mr. Wolf, but you gots the wrong gal. That ain't my name and I don't rightly know what you—

But then he just slump away! He walks outside and I follows him saying Scuse me Mr. Wolf. Nobody else could be bothered with noticing that Howlin' Wolf done left the building. Like time weren't moving none. I finally find him outside behind the jook and, Lord help me, he gots a white man by the neck and he bashing that man's head on the ground saying Let me be for God's sake Let me be!

It look to me like the white man was dead, but then, with blood coming out his ears, he didn't entirely look like a man no more. He looked—

looked like something I can't rightly explain. Whooping like a crane, all twisted up with the devil. Wolf growls to me saying You gots to tell him Jessie! And I scream and everything then was a dark dark dark. I come round and that field hand Negro dropping us off at the house and Mae sayin I don't know what is wrong with you Ella Brown, but you ain't right.

Such a confused right now. Such a confused.

That's all for me, Diary.

God bless and keep everybody and God please show me the way.

I don't know what is wrong with me, Dear God, but I ain't right.

❋

JULY 23 1938
whatever the hell time it is
It's late as a motherfucker and I just saw Ella and Mae sneaking in
She was probably out making time with some man
Why am I even writing this?
She's not my wife.
she's not my wife
she's
not
MY
FUCKING
WIFE!!!

fuck off eli
✽

Dear Diary,
It is Sunday July the 24th in the year of Our Lord 1938.
Lord o Mercy church was a long and hot today! And don't you know
I seen some of them no count Negroes from Crawdaddy's kneeling
down praying this morning. It take a long drive from Caledonia just
to get some religion—ain't my place to judge of course.
God knows I tried to listen good to them gospels extra hard today,
but I just could not shake from my mind what happened last night.
Ain't even really rememberin. Just kind of feel like how a bad dream
sometime linger with you too long.
That Howlin' Wolf—Chester Arthur Burnett what his mama
named him—how come he done what he done, how I seen him do
that man, and ain't nobody said word bout it this morning?
I half figured I'd wake up to word that Howlin' Wolf found dead
in the woods. Lord forgive me, it make my blood to quiver just
saying such.
Could it be that ain't no thing happened at all last night? Did I even
talk to that bluesman? Have I gone funny, Diary? Chester Burnett
got a farm somewhere in Doddsville. Reckon I could go find him
and talk to him a spell. But what in the wide world could I possibly
say? Scuse me Mr. Wolf but didn't I see you bash a white man to
death last Saturday night? And who did you wish me to tell come
find you?
I'd look like a sure enough case for the bug house. That man a
frightful enough without me talking foolishness to him.

Cried in church today, Diary. I know that ain't such a strange cause
it natural to be moved being so close to the Lord and all. This was
a different though. They weren't no tears of heavenly joy. I started
to crying on account of being so confused by what done happened,
but then I got to crying for my Walter. My poor Walter. My love.
Here I go again with the crying, Diary.

I can't rightly say why this catching up to me now of all times.
Just have the feeling that he near me again. I know that he looking
down on me from Heaven and such, but for some reason I feel like

he really and truly near me again! Lordy now I knows sure enough I must be on my last nerve.

Been almost right on five years next month they found my man down by the riverside.

They said he done fell and hit his head on a rocky patch. Yes sir. Fell and hit his head over and over again on them same rocks. God moves on the water, ain't that right Walter? Just like Blind Willie sang it? God moves on the water. Whoo well well.

I know that I done wrote all this down before many a time, but sometime I just got to.

—Our deepest simpathy on your terrible loss, Mrs. Brown—
Well you can be sure I had a mind to tell them where they could stick they damn blasted simpathy!

See what I mean, Diary? I don't never have the mind to get loud or talk improper. It was Walter that always brung that out of me. He always be talking a blue streak bout being who you is and standing up straight. Figure that how he come to fall down on them rocks over and over. Standing up too straight.

God moves on the water, ain't that right baby? And the people come run and pray.

So long for now, Diary. (Lordy! I been writing long time!)
God bless Mrs. D, and Mae, and Alberta and Charlie, and everybody in the house even that crazy painter man in the study.
And God, if you see my Walter, tell him I still loves him and that he still my little school boy.

August 1, 1938
Another fucking Monday.

Thought what the hell. I like keeping a journal, so here I go again.

Lift toss stack. Lift toss stack. Vomit. Lift toss stack. Nigger nigger nigger nigger. Vomit. Every day at work is more excruciating than the last. And, it looks like I'm going to have to spend my every Sunday from now 'til Rapture listening to Reverend Fisher spit fire and brimstone.

"Til Rapture?" This place is really rubbing off on me.

Actually, going to church hasn't been all that bad. It's hotter than a motherfucker, but Lennis and Anna have been introducing me to their fellow parishioners. Real warm, friendly folks. People are sure easy with the invite around here. Supper. Breakfast. Afternoon snack. I wish I had known that when I was living in the goddamn woods.

I have to say, I have met the most courteous, most selfless, most generous people around here. I mean, these people are poor. POOR. And they'll give you anything they can. It's amazing.

Life around the Durning estate is pretty calm. Some guy moved out (Ed I think) and a new guy moved in. Seems like a nice enough fellow. I know I haven't been here that long, but I'm gonna feel kind of funny if people are going to constantly be moving in and out and I keep staying on. Maybe I should think about finding a house for myself. Of course a single guy living alone is probably a little suspicious. Everybody will think I'm gay or something. Maybe I should get married or some shit. As like a dodge or something.

What the fuck am I saying?????!!!!!!
✳

C.

So you may be asking yourself, "If these so-called 'time paths' are so common and plentiful, and most people stumble through them by accident, why don't I know about them?" My answer to that is, *You do.* You may not consciously think about them, but you are perfectly aware of their presence. And more to the point: your innate survival instinct steers you clear of them. If you are in a high rise apartment building on the 18th floor and you're in a hurry to get to the street, the quickest way there is through a window. And yet you don't take that option. "But I've seen windows. I've never seen a time path." Have you looked? If you looked you'd find one. They're everywhere.

✻

August 1, 1938

Okay, I'm back. Just had a burst of inspiration. I'm gonna do our old brownstone. I better get started while my memory still serves me. This is gonna be sweet. I'll get started right after dinner. I wonder if that brownstone is there now? Maybe I could go see sometime.

In five days and sixty-five years or so, Serj will premiere his new exhibit at the Bringham Gallery. I hope to God he doesn't include that stupid *Eyes Over Cali* sculpture. That thing sucks.

Started Mrs. Durning's portrait. This is going to be pretty cool because she doesn't know I've started yet. Found an old photo of her with her husband. Mae did actually. I'm just gonna have to wing it on the coloring. And I actually started with rough sketches. I haven't done that in years. Go figure.

I've been stewing on my *Ella* piece as well. That one's gonna take some time. I wonder if there's anything unkosher about a white painter doing a portrait of an African American woman. I don't think there is. Norman Rockwell did that piece of the little Bridges girl walking to school. *The Problem We All Face* or whatever it's called.

Of course that's years from now.

Did I just compare myself to Norman Rockwell? Good fucking God!

Going nuts.

If I'm not there already.

❄

D.

I've met two other walkers in this jail. (It's funny how we seem to find one another.) One of them is the white boy who gave me this paper. The other is a brother named Amir. Amir Mwate. He doesn't talk like an African, though. More like a Southerner struggling to leave it behind. Unmistakable. He has dreadlocks down to his knees. Not a sight you see too much in 1965. But he swears he hasn't time walked since he was six years old. The white boy gave him some paper too, and he's sketching the folks in our pen ("It seems we're not the only Martians here," Amir said. I don't know what he means). So here we are, all three of us holding writing implements that could easily be jabbed into someone's eye, neck, or stomach. That tells you how stressed these So-Cal cops are. By the time I got here they were processing us in groups of ten. No time for technicalities. More niggers to catch. The white boy looks to be mid-to-late twenties. Amir claims to be 33. Same age as I am. Well, I should clarify that. I am *apparently* 33. I am also *apparently* a Black American man named Jerome Kinnae. I don't really know if that's true. I simply read that that is my name and that's how old I am. This is symptomatic of time walking. It doesn't happen the first time, or the fifth time, or probably even the one-hundredth. But when time walking becomes *what you do,* it becomes *what you are.*

I have no solid memories of a mother or father. I have no idea if I have siblings or any family at all. I don't even know what time I am originally from, although I figure it's probably late twentieth-century. I barely remember my first walk. My first tangible memory is arriving in New York City late 2001 and thinking it was "the future." That was the last I ever considered anything like past, present, future, or anything of the sort. It's all just distance and geography now.

AUGUST 1, 1938

I've been putting off thinking about this.

All right. Here goes.

Yes, I have been talking to Ella. Sure, it was hard at first, for obvious reasons. Also, she's clearly got this whole planned out regimen for dealing with—

You know … people like me, I guess.

That was especially tough considering I'm sure she thinks I'm a fucking weirdo.

Anyway, got past it. Worked it out. I don't think she finds me threatening or anything.

I hope not.

First time I really spoke with her, I almost choked. I saw her cleaning in the parlor, and she's listening to Memphis Minnie, and I just wanted to die.

I came down and she panicked when she saw me, and she goes running over to the Victrola.

"Oh, Mr. Cooper, I's sure sorry. Is the phonograph too loud? I can turn it off—"

So I told her, "No, don't! It's Memphis Minnie. One of my favorites."

"Zat right?" She asked, real nervous and all. I think Mae left then. I can't remember.

"Aw sure," I said. "Ever since I first joined up. The Navy, of course," pointing at all my tattoos. "You know, I've listened to this song in jukes as far away as the Orient if you believe that."

"Well I'll be," she said, but I don't know if she's buying it and I'm starting to sweat. "Missus D don't 'llow no blues music in the house," she continued. "I gots to keep them hidden."

So I told her she could hide stuff, anything she wanted, in my room. Our secret. Trying not to come off like a creep. But I'm *dying*.

"Oh, thas's mighty kind o' you, Missa Coopah."

And I kinda—

lost my cool.

"PLEASE don't call me Mr. Cooper!!!" *Fuck.* "Call me Eli, okay?"

(idiot you fucking idiot DON'T SCARE HER you fucking dumbfuck moron fuckbag imbecile)

It was okay, though.

"Oh, but see now," she said, "Missus D, she quite a particular about us ... " something about first-namin' with the guests is a no-go. I know I'm freaking her out and making her uncomfortable and I just want to fucking DIE.

Regain the cool.

"I see," I said. "Okay. Okay. Well, how about when it's just the two of us, you call me Eli. Fair deal?"

"All right, Mr. Eli. I mean Eli. All right, Eli."

Cool.

She's—

I don't know how to say it. She's different. Different from what I expected. Different from what I'm used to. What does that mean? I don't know. What did I really expect? I don't know.

Could she maybe not be who I think she is?

I don't know.

She's a good dancer, if that means anything at all. She dances to 78s when she's sweeping up.

Sweeping up. Jesus Christ.

I don't understand any of this. Of course. Go figure. I'm just trying to get by. Who said it's all got to mean something? I probably did, but I was probably wrong.

There's something I have been kicking around all week that never would have occurred to me, circumstances not being what they are.

Jessie—and I don't mean this in any negative way 'cause she's forever my baby, forever my angel—

but Jessie,

Jessie Davis-Cooper,

was really just a little kid. Just like me actually. We were little kids together. I didn't realize it then ... But I realize it now. New York was just our playground. "Life" was just fucking playtime. Was our art important? Maybe. Maybe not. Doubt it. Thinking about it now, it didn't really matter. *We were stars.* We thought we were stars. We thought we were big shit, but we were children.

Ella Brown is a grown woman.

She's been dogged and driven. Kicked down and left there, you know? She has suffered. She suffers now. I can see it in her eyes. In her walk. In her tight, thin smile. I see it in the way she squares her shoulders. I see it as she strains her eyes studying the Bible at two in the morning when she doesn't know anybody is watching.

She's more beautiful than anyone I've ever known.

Guess she's not my little bitty pretty one.
But, for whatever it's worth, I've suffered too.

PART THREE

IN DEVILMENT

Lord I'd rather be the devil to be that woman's man.
—Skip James

All "Eyes" On Gifted Young Sculptor

Joel Francisco takes a peek at "This Week In ... "

There once was a time when art mattered.

There once was a time when an individual artistic voice could estrange the realms of color and form, while unifying the whole into one sovereign expression of truth. That voice would scream out to the heavens demanding its own space and vitality. Ladies and gentlemen, the time is nigh again, and the voice has returned. That voice is Serjikan Tobin.

This past weekend, the Bringham Gallery premiered Tobin's first exhibit entitled, appropriately enough, Eyes Over 2001. Both timely and timeless, Eyes Over 2001 progresses through all three of the small gallery's modest show rooms. Most striking was the deliciously cynical yet fluidly transcendent Eyes Over Cali. Here the artist transforms presupposed perceptions of our world into a creation of his own vision and design. The spirit of our times penetrates deeply into the artist's conscience, and Tobin penetrates in kind. Said Tobin, "I hoped to create an atmosphere through line and negative space that refreshes and gives color to our being. Like grasping hands that both throttle and caress."

No less breathtaking are the gorgeously interwoven companion pieces Eyes over Jess and Eyes Over Li. Few, if any, in attendance on that sweltering August 6th could deny the chilling honesty and raw emotion of these two sculptures. The genuine despair expressed in this work couples with a delicate joy that is nothing short of astounding. Jess, with its aura of serenity is dicotomous to Li, which seems to burn with tortured anguish (complete with cryptic blood droplets on the "face" of the figure). The piece representing the late Jessie Davis-Cooper reaches heavenward while the surrogate for missing-in-action Eli Cooper spirals at eye level (to be sure, this is wishful thinking on the part of Tobin).

"Jessie and Eli [Cooper] were the two most gifted, most beautiful people I have ever met," said Tobin through a crack in his voice. "Their absence has left a void that will never be filled. We all loved them very much. I miss them terribly, but they are always with me in my heart."

To use the dreadful cliche "masterpiece" in reference to any portion of this exhibit would be irresponsible, to say the least. That would imply that Tobin has nowhere to go but down, which is most assuredly not the case. Like the inspiration for Eyes Over Li, and of a caliber near to par, this blossoming young talent is sure to be the standard to which all others will be held. Let us just hope that Serjikan Tobin does not follow his comrade's example, and he neither burns out nor fades away. All "eyes" are truly on him now.

The Bringham Gallery will be exhibiting Eyes over 2001 from August 6 to September 11.

Joel Francisco is a nationally syndicated freelance writer and art critic. "This Week In ... " is an exclusive feature of The Asylum Press.

***

DEAREST MR. COOPER,

Words cannot even begin to describe the joy that your wonderful portrait has brought to me. I was sure that you would do a lovely job, but never in my wildest dreams did I suspect that you would create something so heavenly. My stars. Gazing at this handsome young gentleman painted here and, if you will pardon my immodesty, his pretty young bride, simply makes my heart overflow. This young couple looks as though they will be together forever. And now they will be. This portrait is such a tremendous gift. I just cannot thank you enough.

I would like to share something with you and I hope it tickles you as much as it did me—when my dear Ella saw your handiwork for this first time, do you know what she said to me? She said, "Mrs. D, it is a sure enough beautiful." I believe that says it all, don't you?

May God bless and keep you all of your days,

Gladys Durning

E.

I have familiar spots everywhere I go, and people I call "friends." They're not really friends of course, because they don't know me. How can they if I don't? They are simply people of good heart who are willing to open their homes to a mysterious transient. If they'll accept, I often give them some of the money I make guiding the paths. Most don't accept, though. I've become very close with some of these people, such as Reggie and Mabel Tilson of West Point, Mississippi 1938 (I hope I haven't just put them in danger by writing their names). They are the kindest, most giving people I've ever met. Desperately poor, seven beautiful children to feed, Reggie drives a mule plow for barely a few coins, but they welcome me into their home whenever I'm there. I've seen tremendous warmth in the Depression South, and the Tilsons are some of the warmest. They don't even hate the slack-jawed honkies that surround them. "We is all God's chillen, Jerome," Reggie said to me. "Black, white, brown, uh yelluh."

"But they're murderers," I said, talking about the whites down there (and everywhere). He just shrugged.

"I's walkin' wif Jesus, praise God. So I fears no man."

Reggie and Mabel are keeping my bags at their home for me. One reason I need to get back, besides my *cargo*.

✽

Dear Diary,

It is Saturday August the 6th in the year of Our Lord 1938.

Harvest time here. Reckon we can thank old Mr. Whitney for that. Thanks for nothing Mr. Whitney.

I got a mind to be prickly today for some reason I ain't for certain of. Today is a sure enough lovely, but it is hotter than blazes. I feel a might sorry for all the folk out bringing in the crop today.

Nothing too amazing happening. Mae wanting to go barrelhousing tonight of course. And of course she wanting me to go long with her. Loves to ape and clown that girl. Reckon she hunting for a husband but she ain't wanting to look like no loose doney going jooking on her own. That do make good sense but I weary of being her tag along for Heavensake. Now I don't mean to be hurtful, cause Lord knows I loves that girl to pieces, but if she thinking she can go through life like she doing, and getting by on being pretty, well, life going sure enough give her a swift kick to the backside one these days.

I told her if she drag me out again I might have another spell like I done the other night. That shut her up good. For now.

Mrs. Durning been swooning and tearing up all day. Weeping tears of happiness though. She sure ain't sad, Diary. Mr. Eli Cooper—O I gotta remember he said to call him Eli from now on—he done finished painting her picture. That was mighty fast painting! It is a beautiful indeed. He got quite a hand for picture painting and I done told him that I think so. He said Wait til you see the one of you, Ella. Ain't nobody ever done my picture so I feel kind of a nervous but excited too. I asked him why he wanting go and do what he doing. He said Cause you are a dancer, Ella.

I reckon. What that got to do with anything is God's private mistery. Reckon I should of learnt long ago not to wonder why folks do the way they do. Ain't none of my business any old way.

I seen the boy the other day. Night time to tell it true. Too late for to be out by hisself. Reckon he bout six years old by now. He wave to me. I wave. Then he gone. And I cry.

Lord give me strength.

✳

AUGUST 7TH, 1938

Praise Jesus church is fucking over! This period right after church may be my favorite part of the week, because I have a whole seven days before I have to do it again.

I'm quite the hot property today. Mrs. Durning has told "simpleh evrahbody" about the portrait, not too shabby if I do say so myself, and now the town is all "abuzz." A couple of older, and I'm assuming wealthier, couples have asked me to commit their likeness to canvas. If this works out, I might be able to give up plowing and baling all together. That would rule!

I gotta stop writing stuff like that. I have to keep my time and place in check. The other day I was out plowing, and I was sweating like a beast, and I said "This fucking blows!" by accident. *Pffffffft.*

Speaking of "wealthier people," that is a *relative concept* around here. Hard times. Could put a damper on my freelance portrait business.

Maybe I could offer reduced rates or something. Seriously bigtime reduced. This could really pay off if I can get enough people interested. How often do regular folks get the chance to hang their own portraits in their homes? Practically never. This is another good way to make friends as well as a decent chunk of change. Maybe I can make enough money to move to New York!

Question is, do I really want to go now?

More specifically, do I really want to go alone?

Never mind. *Idiot.*

✽

F.

I periodically leave notes for myself in the familiar spots. They all say the same thing: *Jerome Kinnae age 33*. Thing is, I don't know when I first wrote one. Some of them look brand new. Some are yellow and faded. Does that simply mean that they have been yellowing for decades while I walk back and forth through time, and I sometimes find old notes that I just wrote … *or am I not aging?* I don't know. I also don't know if Jerome Kinnae age 33 is really who I am. Perhaps I found someone else's note. Some of them are written in handwriting I don't recognize. This is why I don't see myself ever stopping. I can't fathom settling down somewhere and trying to resume or create a "normal" life. With what? So much of what makes a person who they are is where they are from. And when. When I stopped being from somewhere I stopped being whoever I was. That should make me melancholy, I guess, but I can't honestly miss something that I didn't know was ever there. Not to mention, settling down somewhere sometime would make me a standing target for *Them*.

Who is Jerome Kinnae? I'm a traveling businessman.

❉

AUGUST 8, 1938

Joe and Eddy McDaniel are my first official "clients." I guess I'll stay with them for a couple of days until I get finished or at least get a *feel* for them. I think this is really gonna work out. I've got three more jobs lined up after this one and at least ten others have shown some interest.

I'm enjoying this writing more and more. Someday, maybe when I'm a very old man, I'd like to see about getting it published. I imagine that people would like to read an account of this. I know I would if I wasn't living it. Perhaps at some point I should go back and clean up some of the messier passages. This is for the ages. But what ages?

Okay ...

I'm hesitant to even write this next thing down, cuz I'm trying to pretend like it didn't happen. Heat stroke or something. Delusion. *Collective* delusion. But, if I'm serious about keeping a record of all this, then I have to be honest about everything.
There was some ferocious static at the farm today.

So we're hauling bales. Go figure. Probably midday. Scorching. Thick. Me, Lennis, Jeb, Eugene, all of us. From down in the lower field, I hear someone call my name.

"How's it shaking, Mr. Cooper?"

We all turn around to see this man, Black, probably early-to-mid thirties, tromping up toward us. He's dressed for work, overalls, hat, and I would have just figured him to be a field hand except he's not one bit dirty, and hasn't even broken a sweat.

"You seem to be doing okay for yourself, Mr. Cooper. All things considered. Settling in as best you can. Good good good. Can't be easy in this swamp. Well, are you ready to come home?"
????????

I'm stammering like a moron, "Who ... How do you know—"

"I know you don't belong with these peckerwood hayseeds. I know that."

Lennis growls at him, "You better watch your mouth, boy!"

"No," the guy answers casually, "I'd rather watch *your* mouth, redneck, sucking my dick. Although I'd be afraid of you breaking your rotten-ass teeth on it."

Ohhhhh fuck …

I grab Lennis as he lunges at the man, "I'LL KILL YOU, GOD-DAMN NIGGER! YOU'RE DEAD!" I'm trying to hold Lennis back, but he's built like a fucking ox, and the guy doesn't even blink. He flashes his perfect white teeth at Lennis and says,

"It's called fluoride, cracker. Look into it."

"Come on, Lennis!" I say, "Hold on a minute!"

By this time all the other men are circling this guy, like a pack of wild dogs, and they're gonna tear him to pieces.

"I'LL KILL YOU!!! WORTHLESS SHIT COLORED MON-KEY!"

"Easy there, bubba," the guy's chuckling. *Chuckling!* "Good company here, Eli. And how's that brown sugar, eh? She can come too, for a modest fee."

Shut up, I'm thinking. *Shut up!*

"Come on, Mr. Cooper. You're not scared are you? What are you scared of, huh? Ain't no better there, but it sure ain't no worse. They just traded in the rope and the torch for bullets and billy clubs. For Drug Wars and Death Row. But it's the same ole niggers and the same ole lynch mob! Ha ha ha! Just like *home*, Auntie Em. But now, that's nothing for a *white man* like you to worry about, am I right Mr. Cooper? Nothing for a *white man* to worry about."

He's gonna die. I'm gonna watch this man die right in front of me.

" … Best to be makin' yer prayers, nigger … "

"Plus … there's *big money* on the other side, dawg."

Run, goddamn it, RUN.

"I'll be talking to your agent. We'll be in touch."

And he goes trotting off toward Old Man Morton's house. Lennis breaks free of me and we all go chasing after the guy. But even though I see him just kind of jogging ahead of us, and we're running full tilt … *nobody catches him.* He slips behind the house, and—

GONE. Like he was never there. Everyone's muttering about "Kill the nigger," and "No gawd damn tar baby talkin' ter ME like 'at," and all. Lennis is shaking he's so angry. But fuck …

Where did he go? Nothing but empty field. Where did he go???

When we got back to the bales I looked down on the lower field. All heads down, hard at work. You could feel the fear. Radiating. I could feel it.

It was my fear too.

AUGUST 10, 1938

Quit today.

Old Man Morton is just gonna have to find a new strong back ha ha ha. Good luck to him. I told Lennis about my new gig (I didn't say "gig" though) and he seemed cool with it. "Figg'r you never much liked the work anyhow," he said. "Jest don't you go an' be a stranger, Eli." I told him that I won't. We'll get together on the weekends.

We act like the eighth never happened.
Maybe it didn't.

Here's something. Ella and I have been talking after dinner every night for the past three nights. I play it super cool. No ... funny business. Hell no. We usually just walk around the yard or sit under the tree outside. I'm sure Mrs. Durning knows, but she doesn't seem to mind. She's sure my intentions are pure (that's debatable) and she knows how lonely Ella is.

I mean, I guess Ella's lonely. She doesn't appear to have any friends except for Mae. I suppose she has friends from her church, but she never talks to them or about them.

She told me about her husband. How he died. Seems pretty fucking suspicious to me, but I didn't tell her that. It's not my business. Walter Brown. Sounded like a really cool guy.

"That man had on him a filthy mouth," she said. "My baby was a bullheaded sho' as de day is long. Wouldn't never bow his head in town, he jes' smiled an' tip his hat g'mornin' ta ever'body he pass. White folks ain't lahke him none. He wuhked out on Mr. Mo'ton's farm fo' a spell. He wuhked'd on lossa farms. He weren't fond of it, though. He wanted tuh sang blues fo' a livin' but there wuhn't no money to be made in it, so he jus' done his sangin' in the chu'ch. You ev' hea' uh Blind Willie Johnson? Walter sounded a lil ole bit lahke him."

Have I ever heard of Blind Willie Johnson? HA! I think Walter and I would've been good friends. Sad that such a peculiar accident would take him out. *Yeah, peculiar.* I think I'm gonna avoid the river bank. Just in case.

Back in the day, Walter and Ella used to teach local kids to read and write. "Ev'ry Sund'y affah chu'ch," Ella said. That's super fucking cool! I mentioned to her that she should try and get back into that, but she tensed up stiff as a board and locked her shoulders, so I dropped it.

Ella taught Mae to read and write as well. Well, she tried to anyway. I don't think Mae's too interested in that stuff. I could be wrong, but I think Mae is something of a party girl. You know when Robert Johnson sang, "I gots womens in Vicksburg clean on in to Tennessee, but my West Point rider now hops all over me"? I think he was singing about Mae heh heh heh.

Or maybe it's *Friar's Point*? Oh well. I can't remember.

I wonder what party girls are called around here. I probably shouldn't ask.

I'm stoked as hell about my new employment.

I like spending time with Ella Brown.

This is gonna sound crazy, but, I think I belong here. This town? In this time? Life is pretty fucking good.

Oh, and speaking of Robert Johnson? He's got eight days to live.

DEAR DIARY,
It is Thursday August the 11th in the year of Our Lord 1938.
Today is one perfect! Perfect perfect perfect. Mrs. D gone visiting. I gots all my working done early. Mae off in town doing Lord knows what. All the guests working or looking for work. I gots time for myself and it ain't even two in the morning.
To be truthful, I been in good spirits for the last four days. Reckon things just going my way.
Now you know I ain't been too hopeful for a long time, Diary. Can't reason for certain why I be hopeful now, and I don't rightly know what I hopeful for. Figure the Good Lord just sent a bit of sunshine into my heart.
If so, thank you, Lord. You knows I surely was needing it.
Feeling like I wanting to travel some. Be a rambling gal. Yes indeed! Ain't never done it and I'd like to before I be old and gray. Maybe I will take a trip to see Alberta and Charlie in Selma.
Mrs. D surely won't mind that.
Walter always say he take me to the Big Apple. Who saying I can't go now if even by my own self? I don't hear nobody saying it. Harlem's a calling, yessir! Can't be no more frightful than any other old place. I will take a ferry to New York.

Well, Diary, reckon it won't do to spend my whole free day writing in this here book. I believe I will put some music on the phonograph.
God Bless Mama and Daddy and Walter and Mr. James up in Heaven and God Bless all us down here living life.
✳

AUGUST 12, 1938

The McDaniels have a pretty decent house. Nothing spectacular, but it's not bad. I haven't decided what to charge them yet. They haven't asked.

Awesome dinner last night. Some sort of deep-fried pork thing. I should probably learn how to cook. Maybe not. I've been getting by fairly well so far.

Still working on my pet projects. The *brownstone* needs work. I'm starting over on the *Ella* piece.

Stopped by the Durning House yesterday afternoon to get a change of clothes. It looked like nobody was home, so I was going to go around back and go in through the kitchen door. As I walked around the side of the house, I heard some music playing, but I couldn't make out what it was. I went up to the parlor windows and, Goddamn …

Ella. *Dancing.* Like … she's blessed with lighter air than the rest of us. Free spirit. She's a soul on fire when nobody's around. And man oh man the way the sunlight caught her figure …

Didn't go in. Didn't want to disrupt the moment. Captured it in my mind, though, and I'm committing it to canvas. Hell yeah.

I never did get the change of clothes.

✳

G.

Although I can't disprove them flat out, there are a few hard kept beliefs held by the ignorant who time walk amongst us that I would like to call bullshit on nonetheless. The ones involving "magic," "curses," deals with "the Devil," "fate," "God's will/punishment," "reincarnation," and other such idiocy I won't even dignify. There are others, however, that seem reasonable enough, but are no less wrong and just as dangerous. The most common is the "pocket" theory. As I said before, besides plain old recklessness, it is great distress that often drives a person to ignore that little voice in his subconscious screaming "NOOOOO!!! STOP!!!" and plunge himself headlong down a time path. Pain, grief, fear, rage, the same horror that sends a person flying into heavy traffic or off a rooftop. The same that puts a gun in his mouth and pulls the trigger. So when that person finds himself miles and years from home, still in the throes of whatever agony put him there, his pain is compounded by terror and confusion. He's "trapped" in it. And like any caged animal he will lash out and act out, flinging himself against the bars of his cell, repeating the same destructiveness that caught him there in the first place. This is the perfect method for grabbing *Their* attention, and a real good way to get settled. These people are under the impression that there are "pockets of time," and that they are not to venture past where they "belong." To step out of that time is what gets them trapped, so the thinking goes. Understandable ... but untrue. And *They* perpetuate this untruth because it benefits *Them*. Even many folks sharp enough to realize that it was hopelessness or despair (and a particular breaking point) that sent them barreling through time are still incapable of realizing that it is not the moment itself that they are "trapped" in, but the pain that they are perpetuating themselves. Like I said, this gives *Them* ammunition.

There are no pockets of time. Only your fear can trap you. You have my word on it.

They prey on your fear, your addictions, your ignorance, your desires, and your carelessness. *They* use them against you. Just like all police do. *They* maintain order, and if you are disorderly, rampaging through time causing disarray, you will be exterminated. *They will finish you.* And rightfully so. Of course, not wanting to combat chaos with chaos, *Their* first inclination appears to be to lead troublemakers into situations that will send them over the cliff. Finish them off clean. No questions, no suspicion, everything back to normal, move along, nothing to see here. *They* would rather provide the rope you'll use to hang yourself. Your pet fears and superstitions will knot that noose right up.

That's not to say that *They*'re averse to charging in and tearing you limb from limb if they must. Or dragging you off down the nearest path and chucking you into the abyss. *They* are not called "Hell Hounds" for no damn reason.

Another theory, held by even a lot of experienced walkers, which I don't cop to, is the idea that *They* are unkillable. Nonsense. Despite what many think, *They* are still *human beings.*

"But I've killed a few!" some people have said to me, "and seen the very same ones alive again!" Sorry, I don't buy it. *They* are able to dress themselves in myriad forms, and to appear as one that's already been killed is just another tool of fear. To suggest otherwise is to tell ghost stories.

Another ridiculous notion to which some cling, even those who should know better, is the idea that some walkers are able to force their way into another time *after death.* That they can actually be *born again* as themselves. Or even, according to a few half-wits, as someone else entirely! "They don't even know who they really are," so it's said (and always in hushed tones), "but you can spot them because they carry the scars of their deaths with them." Oooooooo! Throw some more wood on the campfire, it's getting chilly out here. My question is always: if they're in a brand new body and have no recollection of who they "really are" ... then how or why should they be anyone but who they believe themselves to be? I've never been killed and I'm not even who I "really am." Ignorance.

(I must admit that in my darker moments I've given this idea some consideration. More than it deserves, I'd say. The *cargo* I've mentioned that is currently in Mississippi 1938 is a young man who I followed from New York 2001. I was originally interested in him simply because I thought I could make some decent money guiding him back. He's an artist of some renown in select circles and getting him home safely seemed like a win-win proposition for all concerned—me most of all. But the more I watched him the more I got the feeling that he's not who he says he is. Or even who he thinks he is. I can't explain it … it's just a feeling I have. And it's pressing on me to get the fuck out of this jail, back to New York, and on to Mississippi with all due speed. Really this concept is too absurd to give it any credence. But I believe that we have instincts for a reason, and they're to be ignored at our own peril.)

AUGUST 14, 1938

About noon or so.

Robert Johnson gave his final performance last night. He's laid out dying somewhere right now. Probably just my imagination, but I feel like it has cast a dark vibe over the day.

"You may bury my body down by the highway side. So my ole evil spirit kin catch a Greyhound bus n' ride."

Went to church with the McDaniels. They're all excited because I told them I'd be finished with the painting tomorrow. I'm going to have supper at the Martins' tonight. Man, that's good stuff.

Think I'm gonna go for a walk. I probably wouldn't recognize a magnolia if I saw one, but I'm gonna do a couple of flower sketches. Who knows? I'll see what I come up with.

Just call me the Mississippi Van Gogh.

❈

DEAR DIARY,

It is Sunday August the 14th in the year of Our Lord 1938.

Real nice sermon today. Don't remember it too clear, but it was a right nice.

I feel like a foolish, Diary. And more than a bit not thinking right. Still feeling light in my step like I been, but I been feeling more lonesome the past couple days than usual. I just feel if I stopped being here tomorrow ain't nobody take a notice. Now I don't mean to be sorry for myself. Lord in Heaven knows Job and plenty others had worse off than I got. Just that I—

I don't often got nobody to keep my company. Reckon I could talk to Mae, but she just gets to yacking on bout this man or that man. I gots half a mind to write a letter to Alberta, but she can't read none so what the good is that?

Eli Cooper—Eli—he gone off to do his picture painting. I enjoys talking to him quite a good deal. Seem he the only person knowing I be alive most the time.

Lordy I shouldn't even write such.

Ain't going say no more bout it.

God bless.

August 14, 1938

I'm out for a stroll around West Point. I appear to have wandered a bit too far, because I ended up walking down this dirt path without realizing it. That's where I am now. I've never seen this road before, but hell, I'm no expert on the area. I'm really taken by how this road plays geometrically with the trees on either side. Following the vanishing point back, it's practically a perfect triangle. So anyway …

I had stopped to do a quick sketch, and from out of nowhere, this little kid runs into me at top speed. He was carrying about eight sheets of paper, and they all go flying this way and that. *God. This boy really looks familiar.* Huffing and puffing down the road after him was a much older man. Probably the boy's grandfather.

"Lafeyette!" The old man hollered, "Lafeyette! Damnit chile I done tole you ta slow down, now lookit whut ya done! So long's you Black, you best ta mind me, boy. I'll warm up yo' lil backside fo' ya!"

By this time, I was down trying to help the boy pick up his papers. *They're drawings!* Damn good ones at that, from what I saw at first glance.

"It's okay, sir," I said. "No damage done."

The old man absolutely would not look me in the eyes. Very disconcerting.

"I is (*huff huff*) sho' sorry fo' da boy, suh," he stammered, "Sho' sorry. Da boy, (*huff huff*) he simple, suh. But he a good boy. Cain't do no work, don't hardly even talk none, but he don't mean no harm, suh. His mamma (*huff*) pass on, an' I gots ta look aft' 'im. He don't do nothin' but make dese pit'chers, but he a good boy, suh. He jus' simple 'sall."

"Quite all right, sir. Quite all right. May I see your drawings, Lafeyette?"

"Well," the old man said nervously, "Show de man yo' pit'chers, Lafeyette."

So the boy handed me his pages. *Astounding.* This young fellow could not be more than seven years old, and his use of space and shading … I don't know if I've ever seen anything like it. Almost makes me want to pack it in. Most of his work's just abstract shapes and angles.

One piece, though, was a near-perfect perspective still of a rope hanging from a tree branch.

I've seen this before …

And what's this? A monster. A multi-spotted creature—metal spikes, hooks, and chains in its face—face dripping with blood—long twisted snakes hanging from its head.

Hmm … oh yeah …

The old man looked on in embarrassment.

"See, I tole ya he jus' a simple boy, suh. He got de 'magination. Well, we mus' git goin' now."

"This is great work," I told the boy. "I'm an artist too, Lafeyette, and I want you to know that you have a lot of talent. Would you mind making a trade? I'll give you one of my pictures if you give me this monster drawing."

Gotta cover the ass.

The boy nodded in agreement and pointed to the road sketch I had just finished. At the bottom right corner of my *portrait,* he scribbled in his "signature." A pair of eyes and a crooked smile. *Cool fucking signature!* Way cooler than mine—Li81438. Oh well.

"You've got a really gifted boy here, sir," I told the old man as Lafeyette and I swapped masterpieces.

"Well, whut do ya say to de man, Lafeyette?"

"Thank you, suh," Lafeyette said with a twisted little grin. "An' it wuz nice to make yo' 'quaintence. Again."

And off they went.

I should keep on walking.
See what else runs into me.

DEAR DIARY,

It is still August the 14th in the year of Our Lord 1938.

I just been setting here all day resting my mind. Ain't really got nothing new to write, just passing my time away. Mae come in here earlier saying hello. I says hello, and she starts to shifting on her feet all nervous like. I says, What is it, child? And she says, I worrying bout you, Ella. You a young woman. You gots to have more a life than this. You ought not be trapped in one moment, Ella. I be worried you ain't rightly living at all, and well, if it be on count of your husband, you know he be wanting you having gladness in your heart.

Reckon he would, I say.

And she say, What was it Walter call you, Ella? His little bitty pretty one? He would not be wanting his little bitty pretty one so blue all time.

I done told her she right. God bless her.

HOLY SHIT!!!!

Serves me right for tempting fate!

So I'm walking along down that same dirt path, and I see this ramshackle little cottage off the way a bit, and this old woman sitting on the porch.

"Afternoon, ma'am," I called to her.

She sat up real straight turning her head from side to side—guess she's blind or something.

"Who that? Who there?" she asked in a panic. "Whut' choo want wit me? Who there?"

"Nobody, ma'am. Nothing. I didn't mean to startle you. I just wanted to say good afternoon, and—"

She totally freaked out. She started screaming and shaking her head and waving her index finger in the air.

"Cain't be you, boy! Cain't be you! I rec'nize th' tone uh yo' voice, but cain't be you! You's DEAD, boy! YOU'S DEAD, BOY!!!!!!!!!!!"

I said good day and got the hell out of there.

I told Lennis and Anna about it when I got back. Lennis thought it was funny.

"Don't let that poor ole nigra spook ya, Eli," he laughed. "They can get crazy with voodooin' and such, but it don't mean nothin'."

Okay.

✻

DEAR DIARY,

It is Sunday evening August the 14th in the year of Our Lord 1938.

Reckon I got a mind for some Bible reading tonight, but it is late and my eyes is weighing down low.

Eli come home tonight looking like he done come face to face with Lucifer hisself asking, Can we talk? I ask, What the matter and he told me this crazy tale of him coming cross this old Negro woman who call him The Dead Boy or some such thing. I must say it did not make much earthly sense to me. Sort a funny to tell God's honest truth. And he done the voice real good too!

But you know I feel right sorry for him. Poor Eli. I know how he feeling. Half a crazy and can't even trust your own God given eyes. So I done told him bout my dealings at that jookjoint. My dealings with Howlin' Wolf some Saturdays ago.

Well, Diary, he bout to lost his mind when I done told him my story! He jump right up and use the Lord's name in vain. So I says back to him, Now I hope you don't mean no blasfemy by saying such. He says, No I don't mean that, but I have to meet him! I have to see Howlin' Wolf. I think he can sort things out for me!

Lord have mercy.

I told him that Chester Burnett, under some name or another, usually playing somewhere just bout every Saturday night if you gots the mind to look. So he says, This Saturday I will find the man. He knows me, Eli say.

I done told him, You going go walking into a colored man's jook you must be a plum crazy! Plus, I told him, the Devil here in Mississippi. And I for certain his name Chester Burnett.

Eli says, Ella, Howlin' Wolf ain't the Devil in Mississippi. Thank you much, but I will take my chances.

So then I says to him, Well, I gots to look out for all God's children, and Lord only knows what evil the Wolf gots in store.

So he say, What you saying? You saying you care for me Ella?

Reckon I do, I say. Reckon I do.

I care for you too, he say.

That's what he say.

Reckon I do care, Diary.
The Lord sure do work in misterious ways.
God bless all us poor lost sheep.
And please show us the way.
✻

H.

Path guiding is my bread and butter. I charge people a modest fee for taking them safely from one time to another. I don't really have a standard rate, and I base my price on A) the risk of the particular path, B) the ability of the client to pay, C) the risk the client himself brings [Is he being hunted? Is this a first walk? A "back home" walk? etc.], D) whether or not I am going to have to find him and bring him back to where we started. I added that last stipulation after Robert Johnson.

For those of you who don't know, Robert Johnson was a famous blues singer. The legend among non-walkers reads like this: Robert was a piss-poor guitar picker from the Mississippi Delta. Fueled by the desire to become a great musician, plus an abundance of youthful *fuckitall*, Robert sold his soul to Satan (well … that's partly right anyway). You can go ahead and add a dash of grief over the recent death of his wife and unborn child to that emotional stew as well. Truth of the matter; he was *hardly* a poor guitarist. In fact, he was brilliant when I met him. But he wanted more, and was willing to do anything to be the best.

It was 2:23AM when I met Robert out on the highway (Mississippi, 1934, and I was wearing a *digital watch*). "Mista Kinnae, sir," he said, "I's ready to sell my soul." We had a good laugh.

From New York we walked to Chicago 1949, Memphis 1972, Austin 1987, and everywhere we went, Robert managed to scrounge up enough money to keep paying me. So I kept guiding him. We weren't in Chicago but an hour and a half and he had already balled some girl in the back room of a tavern and gotten into a fistfight. But he was dead serious about his music, and soaked up whatever was going down in every town and every time we went. He was like a human tape recorder: hear a song one time in a noisy, crowded room, and could play it note for note. (I have a theory that he actually stole licks from the very musicians who cite him as their influence.)

Finally Robert decided to head back home, and was sure he could go it alone. Catastrophic mistake. *They* caught his scent somewhere along the line, which, given his complete inability to keep a low profile, did not surprise me.

I saw him once more before his time ran out at Three Forks. I caught his show at a little juke house outside Doddsville. "I's a sure enough murdered man, Mista Kinnae," he whispered to me, his eyes sunk deep in his head. "A sure enough murdered man." I'm not often sad—I don't usually feel much of anything at all—but I was sad that night. As I stood there watching and listening to him play … I could not believe my ears. Song after song about "Hell Hounds," "Spooks," "Enemies" overtaking him. Right in front of all those people, *spilling his guts*. There were three of *Them* there that night, dressed to the nines, and I could see *Them* shaking and twitching, barely able to keep human. To this day I'm amazed *They* didn't just charge him right then and there and rip him to bits. He even sang a song about "walking side by side with the Devil," and he smiled at me. I smiled back. Our own little joke. I never saw him again.

He had told a couple of other young blues men about his travels and the skills he'd picked up along the way. Naturally, all of them ran out and did it. *All of them died straight away.* Well, all but a singer named Chester Burnett. Big boy: strong as bull and twice as wild. Chester navigated the path a number of times entirely on his own with little trouble. But he's one of the worst rampagers I've ever seen. The very first one of *Them* he met, he murdered on the spot—head hacked clean in half with a garden tool. After Robert was killed Chester quit walking for good (although I've heard he did guide a lady once more), but it was too late. *They* hounded, hunted, and haunted him the rest of his life. He has crossed paths with that white artist from New York, my *cargo*, and I've offered to guide them both safely for a fair price (sometimes I feel that this low-rent capitalism is the only thing keeping me human). Only time will tell how that goes, but right now I'd just as soon not do it. No more musicians for me. The ones who aren't imbeciles are reckless, and the rest are shit-house crazy.

✳

AUGUST 14, 1938

Late as hell.

All praise to who-the-hell-ever is pushing the buttons!!!

I understand everything!

At last it all makes perfect fucking sense!

Mississippi. Center of the goddamn universe.

I'm painting again. Hell yes I am!

And dig this: I am actually going to see Howlin' Wolf in his prime in all his devastating glory perform live in person in the goddamn flesh this Saturday night!

Say dreams don't come true? Go fuck yourself.

I never want to leave this moment.

I gotta spell Heaven with four little "s"es, four little "i"s, two little "p"s, and one big-ass "M."

HALLEFUCKINLUJAH!!!

✻

The Clarion-Ledger

News In Brief

SATURDAY AUGUST 20 BELZONI, MISS: Popular Negro nightspot the Harlem Tavern was the setting for a near-riot last evening after a performance by local race musician Chester Burnett—better known as The Howling Wolf. Witnesses report that Burnett himself and an unidentified white companion assaulted a small group of well-dressed patrons with liquor bottles. The already overexcited Negro audience quickly transformed into a brawling mob, which spilled out into the street leaving extensive property damage and several injured. By the time local police officers arrived, however, neither Burnett nor his companion were anywhere to be found. Their mysterious victims, identified only as one white male and three colored males in matching gray suits, had also fled.

Said one concerned citizen, "I ain't had no problem with them people so long as they keep to their side of the road. But if they're going to act like bad children, I say let's treat them like bad children. This sort of business is a black eye on the community, pardon the joke."

ASSOCIATED PRESS

PART FOUR

HELLHOUNDS ON YOUR TRAIL

Hey hey, baby, I got blood in my eyes for you.
—MISSISSIPPI SHEIKS

To: Mr. Marcus Sims c/o Sims & Sims Inc.
Private

Dear Mr. Sims,

I hope you will forgive this rather antiquated method of communication, but I do so love writing letters. My reason for writing you is this: It is my understanding that you have lost some, shall we say "property," that is very dear to you. Although I had no hand in "its" disappearance, I believe I can return it to you in relatively stable condition. You realize, of course, that this favor I am willing to do for you will not come cheap. I am confident, however, that you won't mind the fee.

I cannot go into any further detail, for time is of the essence, and you no doubt would not accept any explanation I offered. Just trust, you will not be disappointed.

It is now August 21, 2001, 4:27AM. By the time you read this, I will be standing in Central Park. I will call you on the telephone at exactly 8:30AM to let you know I am on the job and on my way. Do not try to track me or find me. You will not.
Sincerely,
Jerome Kinnae

P.S. Do you think you could handle representing a legendary musician? If so, I may have a special bonus for you as well.
P.P.S. Regarding payment, I suppose we will have to work this C.O.D. Just don't leave me hangin'.

❃

To: serjnamie@yahoo.com
From: marc@marcsims.com
Sent: 8/21/01
Subject: nutjob

Serj!
Did you get that letter I faxed you? What the hell is all this about? Who is this fucking Kinnae crackpot? Do you know him? What musician is he referring to? If this is about that Sleepy-whoever shit band, I say fuck 'em. They got what they paid for.
Marcus

August 21, 1938

Gotta be about noon or so. Been in Belzonia all night. Just got in. Goddamn.

I just have to—

I'll write more when I have my wits about me.

I.

You may at this point be thinking that the safest way to make it through a time path is to find an experienced walker to guide you. Absolutely NOT. I wouldn't trust a life-timer to guide an old woman one block to church on Sunday morning. Remember: these are people whose entire existence is based around lying, deceit, theft, and sometimes murder. They are homeless, rootless, completely self-oriented, and not bound or beholden to any laws you recognize. Not to mention, many of them are so far removed from whoever they once were that they've practically lost all sense of what it means to be *human.* Some of them don't even look human any more (which is why I say thank "god" for my petty greed. It's keeping my blood warm and my posture erect).

Associating yourself with a life-timer does have its benefits, though. Not the least of which is they'll be able to tell when *They* are on the prowl well before you will. For brief moments, *They* are able to "ripple" seconds and minutes around *Themselves,* which will appear to you like everything has become dull and slow. But actually it's *Them* moving extremely fast. Experienced walkers will spot the ripples and can "ride" them just like *They* do. (Few non-walkers will ever notice any of this, but they would see it plain as day if they bothered to pay attention ... and knew what to look for.)

I hate to even write this next thing because it may very well boot me right out of the job market, but I've recently come to understand why life-timers are so dangerous. It's because novice time-walkers, first-timers, and rampagers are goddamned *contemptible,* and they fuck everything up for the rest of us. They *deserve* to be taken, used and abused. And many of them deserve to be settled. Perhaps that's cruel of me and it's just cynicism and world-weariness talking. But I'll be guiding somebody, and the sudden urge to rip his throat out or walk him right into the nothing will overwhelm me. Not long ago I was guiding a little Chicano woman back home to Dallas, 1992. She'd lost her baby in a car accident. She had, in a fit of grief, tossed herself off a rooftop into an alleyway, and ended up with a concussion on a hog farm in Ohio, 1910. "Oh Dios Mio," she whined the whole fucking walk, "I can hear my baby a-screaming for me! Mama! Mama! And I can't stop falling and falling and falling! Trapped in 'iss moment for all time, Oh Hey-zeus, Maria, y Ho-say!" I was *disgusted*. It's people like her who bring out *the Dogs* ... or worse yet, set forth a particular course of time that's significantly worse than what would have happened had they not meddled. *Kill her, Kill her, Kill her,* I thought. *Lead her pretty ass to a prison farm. She wanted to die anyway.* But I didn't, and I'm glad (I hope I *never* do such a thing). Now that she's home I doubt she'll ever time walk again. And it's not my place to settle people.

❋

August 21, 1938
Still kinda shaken.

It was lik—
ohgod
   I can already feel last night fading from my memory. Like I just woke from a dream.
I better write this fast.

   I knew Ella wouldn't tell me anything, so I asked Mae if she knew where Howlin' Wolf would be playing tonight.
   "Ha'lem Tav'n," she said. "In Belzonia." *Belzonia … Sounds familiar …*
   "You wanna go?" I asked her.
   "No 'fense, Missa Coppah. But Ah cain't go to no jook wit'choo. Jus' cain't."
   "I understand. Thank you, Mae."
   "Wolf goin' change yo' lahfe, suh."
   "That's what I'm counting on."

   I talked Lennis into driving me, but he was suspicious as all git-out. He asked me what business I had going all the way to Belzoni (that's what Lennis called it. Without the "a"—don't know which it actually is). Told him it's a spiritual thing. That was probably the wrong thing to say. We barely talked the whole drive there. Should have just told him I was going bass fishing.
   I'm not exactly sure where he dropped me off. The last sign I saw was for Tchula, but that was some distance back. *Jesus, what a run-down area.*
   By some wandering miracle, I finally did stumble across the place. H RLEM TAV RN.
Guess this is it.
   There was a really good band playing when I walked in. Classic delta string band. You'd have thought I was a leper shedding limbs by how folks were acting around me, though. I told the barkeep that

I was a rep from Decca Records. Got me a shot of whiskey on the house.

"Well suh, it mus' be a special night fo' da Wolf," he said. "Dem gentl'mens ov' dere? Dey from some rek'id comp'ny z'well."

He pointed to four guys in matching pin-striped suits. Three Black men, one white. They raised their glasses to me and smiled. Creepy. Familiar. Word spread pretty quickly about all the "big time music people" in attendance. I downed the shot, then ordered a gin on the rocks.

They didn't have any rocks.

All of a sudden, the room fell dead silent. I was expecting some sort of *Ladies and Gentlemen, Mississippi's very own …* but there was nothing of the sort. Some fellow casually got up behind the drums, and another fellow picked up his guitar.

I didn't turn around, but I heard a voice whisper in my ear, "This moment … Don't never forget it."

Then, out of the blue, this gigantic man appeared on stage. He glared out into the audience with his eyes rolled up like he was possessed … hypnotized … something …
Goddamn it! I knew it was him! Howlin' fuckin' Wolf!

The veins in that man's neck bulged and throbbed. His massive fists clenched. Lips locked, eyelids now locked. Jaw locked. A polytonal hum began to vibrate through the speakers with a steady crescendo. Louder now. Louder still. Steady. Steady.

Somebody hollered, "Brang it, boy!"

"Brang it on home!"

"We's needin' it 'bout now!"

Wolf pursed his lips and from somewhere deep in the center of the earth, a thousand coyotes howled.

The reverb from the PA buzzed, squealed, popped, and craaaackled …

"Whoooahh I axed her fo' watuh'/ Whoooahh an' she brought me gasoline/ dat's duh terriblest woman-ooooo/ dat I evuh seeeeeeeen!"

The whole room swayed one-and-two-and-three-and-four and Wolf howled. Everbody howled.

"Sang da song, chile! Sang it!" they yelled.

"Whoooahh da chu'ch bell tonin'/ Whoooahh da hearse gone drivin' slow/ I hope my babeeeeee/ Don' leave me no mooooohh'!"

This moment … Don't never forget it.

The rest of the set was a blur. I didn't recognize too much of the music, but it didn't matter. *Never in my life …*

Howlin' Wolf in the prime of his youth …

Good God, what can I say? Few people of my time have ever heard this. No one my age has.

Hell with that. *This* is my time. My life … twisted and all.

After the show was through and the devastation total, Wolf stepped from the makeshift stage, lumbered on to the end of the bar, and sat down. I watched him for a few minutes, as I gathered up my moxie. Women slunk up to him. He'd nod and smile. They'd slip him a little piece of paper. He'd tuck it into his shirt pocket. Eventually, I headed down. Stood behind him in silence for a few painfully long seconds.

"Good evening, Mr. Burnett. Very fine performance. So what are you drinking, sir?"

He chuckled. Chuckled that deep raspy chuckle. Hell yeah.

"Whiskey straight up," he said. "Make it uh double. Ya know, mah frens call meh Chess. Mah good frens call meh Wolf. Have uh seat, Missah Coopah."

"My friends call me Eli. My good friends call me Li. And to answer your question, I'd have to say that I'm more of an explorer than a mad scientist. Now let me ask you; This here's the Harlem Tavern. You ever been to Harlem?"

"Aw mercy me!" he laughed, "Reck'n I have … jes' not yet. Whoo Lawd!"

Suddenly, Wolf stopped short and his eyes scoped the room. He didn't move his head, but he seemed to take it all in.

"Lot's changed since that night, fren," he continued, "Good to see ya took all 'at shit out cho' face n' cut dat mess offa yo' head. Li, eh? Sound lahke a bluesman's name. Red Dev'l Li. Hah hah. Yes indeed."

"Red Devil Li," I said flattered as hell. "Just like the kind *she mixed your drink* with."

Wolf's eyes became softballs bulging from his face. He sniffed his whiskey suspiciously.

"What you say?" He panicked, "*Who* mix my drank? This here drank? Who *she*? Who tryin' ta kill meh now?"

"No no," I said. "In the song. Your song, "Commit a Crime." '*You mixed my drink/ with a can of Red Devil Lye …* '"

"Ah ain't wrote no song lahke 'at."

"You will."

"Hmm … Ah reckon. Hey. Lookahere. I need ya do sump'n fo' meh. Read 'is."

He pulled a crinkled up letter from his left front pants pocket. It read:

To: Chester Arthur Burnett. Doddsville, Miss.
Private

Dear Mr. Burnett,

Please meet me in West Point on August 29th. You know where. Night time is the right time.

Sincerely,
Jerome Kinnae

"Hmm," he murmured. "West Point … "

"Does this mean something to you, Wolf? Who is this guy?"

"Never met da man," he said. "Mus' be anoth' one watchin' meh."

Guess we talked for about forty-five minutes. He did anyway. I didn't say too much. This is Howlin' Wolf talking. I'm gonna listen.

"Reckon you huh'd bout Dusty?"

"Robert Johnson?"

"Robert Johnson, yessuh."

"Yeah. I *already* knew. Ya know?"

Po' Bob. Finally did die on Tuesd'y. Rice Miller an' mah sista, they was 'ere at Three Fo'ks wid him. Sonny Boy said befo' he died, he's down on hands 'n knees barkin' like a dog. Now that's plum out of it. But I know'd dey'd git 'im. Reckon dey git me too."

"What do you mean 'I knew they'd get him,' Wolf?"

He leaned back and exhaled deeply. I don't know if you'd call it *fear*, but something was weighing heavy on his eyes.

"You huh'd Bob's tunes. *'Hellhound's on mah trail/ Blues fallin' lahke hail/ mah do' knob's turnin'/ mus' be spooks around mah bed.'* Robuht slipped through de pocket jus' lahke Ah did. Jus' lahke you did. Dis'peared—came back gooder at playin' den when he took off. 'At's why folks say he solded his soul ta Satan. Shit. Ain't no Satan but da one starin' in yo' mirruh. *But them thangs is real.*"

Wolf nodded his head towards the four men in the fancy threads. The four all smiled and nodded in unison, hoisting their cocktails.

"Ah don't know who o' what they is. Demons, spir'ts, but dey don't take ta folks leavin' dey own tah'me. All night dem's knock an' scratch at mah do'. Whisper in mah window. To'ment me in mah dreams. Now dey come to mah shows. See dem fo' sittin' 'ere grinnin' at me? Ain't human, dem creach'es. That slick nigguh on da lef' he come ta my fahm bout a week affah you n' me met in yo' tahme. Sayin' he wantin' meh ta sign a contrac' fo' ta make rec'ds. Now Ah don' know why, but my fuhst mind wus ta jab mah blade clear int' his neck! An' at's jus' what Ah done! Dere he wus jus' a-squealin' an a-bleedin' lahke a stuck pig sprayin' blood all on mah cotton, and I's sayin', 'Lawdy what to do now?!' But dere he is. Smilin' dat dev'l smile." Big gulp of whiskey. "Dat hunky next tuh 'im—Done smashed his head in Caledonia. Yo' little sugar mama saw meh do it. Rec'nized her from ... Scair't her haf' to deaf, Ah s'pose."

An astoundingly gorgeous lady walked up behind us and whispered in his ear like I wasn't even there, *"Howlin' Wolf, you touches me deep inside. You's even in my bad dreams an' I likes it."*

Wolf just smiled and nodded, and she went slinking away. He immediately reattached his stare on the four men.

"Dem thangs killed lil Dusty," he continued without missing a beat. "Dey goin' kill meh too. But Ah'll fight. Ah ain't 'fraid ta break no crackuh's skull. Ain't nobody mak'n strange fruit out dis Mississippi son."

I couldn't tell if he was drunk, paranoid, out of his mind, or all that combined. *"They,"* whoever they are, they don't ever kill him. He isn't killed. Chester Burnett died when I was two. Heart failure—he's a big motherfucker! But he lives to be a relatively old man. And famous. They build a statue of him in West Point. His face ends up on a goddamn stamp for chrissake! Of course I know I shouldn't tell him that. It could seriously alter the natural course of time. Disrupt the future ... and that could be cataclysmic.

Fuck it. I told him anyway.

He wasn't comforted, though. He just stared into his drink and shook his head.

"Den dey ain' nev' goin' let me be. Jus' goin' haunt me fo' all mah day."

"Wolf, how'd you end up in my time? How'd you end up in—"

"Cain't say. Don't know. I don't rightly know how t'all happ'ned. I am jus' a country boy. Ain't even a rambler lahke all th'others. Ah be twen' nine yea's old 'ere soon an' Ah ain't nev' been too fah from de delta. 'Cept fo' when I slipped through dat damn pocket. Real cocky Ah reckon. Po' boy long way from home, but da world cain't do meh no hah'm. Lawd Lawd."

He shook his head, downed his whiskey, and ordered another.

"Time ... " I whispered to myself.

"Strange mem'ries uh thangs I didn't r'call befo'. Mem'ries uh thangs 'at ain't happ'ned yet. Heav'n only know. ONLY Heav'n know. Tahme. Iss all fouled up. Reckon we jus' keep meetin' here an then. Trapped forev' in dis moment. 'Til dey get one us. Or BOF' us."

"Can I get back?"

"Mississippi got dat hahd pull, fren. T'on't mattuh now no how. Any which way, dey goin' affah YOU now. Dey's on you. Mind yo'sef, cuz dey's comin'. See 'em smile at'choo? Dey's comin'."

Wolf stood up and leaned over to my ear.

"Don't know how dey comin' tuh you, but dey will. Came lahke spooks 'n hellhounds on Dusty's trail. Now ya know dey cain't come at da Wolf lahke no hound, but dey come at me all da same. Lahke yo' wuhst dreams dey come. Ya stepped outta tahme. If'n Ah don' see ya no mo', Red Dev'l Li, iss been mah honah."

I yelled out as he headed towards the door, "Wolf! Wait! I need to ask you—!"

"Ah cain't answer nuthin'. Mind yo' back, cus dey on you. Lahke *hellhounds*. It's da bluesman's death."

But I'm ... I'm a neo-post-impressionist.

Just as I started after him, around they came. The Pin-Stripes. The four of them.

I could hear them. Muttering.

> "We gonna make up this here contract or we gonna
>   make up yo' dying bed."
> "Gotta keep it all in order here."
> "Can't go slipping off as you choose."
> "Johnson got a hellhound easy as pie."
> "It's fininshed."
> "He's finished."
> "You're finished."
> "Can't never hide."
> "Can't never hide."
> "Can't never hide."
> "So you're the tail dragger. Ain't that right, Wolf?"

I could smell it in the air. Evil going on. Wolf hunched his back, grabbed one of them, smashed him in the jaw, and snarled.

"I's gonna r'member you sorry fuckahs WHO AH AM!"

That moment, the Harlem Tavern exploded.

Fists flying. Women screaming. My eyes burned. I could taste my blood. A table smashed through the liquor rack. Wood splintered. Glass shattered. Through the melee, I could see the barkeep loading his pistol.

Then, like BOOM! everything … slowed … to a crawl …

I saw Wolf jab a broken bottle into "the hunky's" face. Hunky spat and convulsed and whooped like a crane. His body twisted like frizzling meat. "The slick nigguh" turned his bleeding eyes dead on me and,

I can't even—

he screeched,

screeeeeeeched—

"We settled you once, boy! Reckon we'll settle you again! You's dead boy, but we'll settle you again! Stepped outta yo' time, boy! WE WILL SETTLE YOU!!!"

Tearing out the door, I ran into the darkness with the cacaphony fading behind me. I could feel my own warm blood spilling from my nose, seeping through my shirt. *Was I hit?*

My spiritual journey.

I have no idea how I made it home.

✻

DEAR DIARY,

It is Sunday August 21st in the year of Our Lord 1938.

My goodness what a morning! Mae and me was walking up the yard coming from church, when we sees Eli just a-stumbling and staggering up to the house. At first I thinking he drunk, but the closer I gets I notice that he bleeding! Well, we brang him into the kitchen and help him to clean up some. I check his nose and it weren't broke. Lord have mercy, I told that fool man, I done told you that you ought not go to that jook but you went anyhow and now just look!

I think Mae just bout to fainted when I said that! We don't never talk to guests—or nobody for that matter—with such a cross tone, but Eli, he my good friend.

He said You right Ella. You right, but I met the Wolf. I met Howlin' Wolf.

Well then, I ask him, Did Mr. Wolf tell you who Jessie?

I know who Jessie is, he say. Scuse me I gotta go.

Then he went off to his room. He just left to go to Mr. Martin's house for supper.

Mae says to me, You fuss over that man, Ella. You fuss over him more than you fuss over other guests. I just hoping—

Mae, you best to keep a civil tongue in your head! I says, That nonsense!

Alright then, she say. Alright, but you knows the language I be talking.

That girl coming at me with such mess. Some nerve, Diary. I tell you what. Some nerve.

J.

And as I've said before, I'm no expert on time walking myself. Just when I think I've figured it all out, I'm taken by surprise. Example:

Mississippi, 1938. I'd accompanied Reggie to the plantation where he works. I knew that white New York artist was working on an adjacent field, trying to blend in with the just-plain folks. So I go right up to him and introduce myself. All his cracker compadres start circling me, talking all their "nigger" jive, so I start fucking with them. *Hard.* I must have been out of my mind talking that shit, there wasn't a path for miles. But I'm giving it to them right to their red, splotchy faces and their blood is boiling. Finally I take off toward the nearest farmhouse laughing my ass off, and they are *burning* after me. Now, I'm a pretty fast sprinter and in mighty fine shape if I do say so, but by all rights they should have caught me. But just as they're gaining ground, there's a quick ripple … and I fly ahead. I turn around, and they're all milling about like ants in cold molasses. I quickly scan the area for *Them* … but it's just me there. So I took off toward the nearest path, which led me to Fort Collins, Colorado, '82, and straight on to Watts, '65. And here I am.

❋

AUGUST 21, 1938

I feel like I've been hit by a wrecking ball. I should be helping Lennis bring in wood for the stove, but Anna wouldn't hear of it.

"You've had a hard night, Eli," she said. "You just go sit yourself down on the porch and make a picture or whatever you please."

So I'm doing just that. I don't go anywhere without my journal and my sketchbook. Godamn it! My style! *I've lost my style.* I don't know how it happened, but the patented Eli Cooper look appears to be MIA. *If Edvard Munch and Jackson Pollock had a child* and so on. I've turned into a fourth rate hack. Oh well. People seem to like it. I just need enough money for a train ticket out of this mudpit.

It has only been a couple of hours since I wrote out everything that happened last night, but … even reading it, I barely remember it. It's like I dreamed it or something. No one talks about it either. There was a blurb in the *Clarion-Ledger* this morning, but no one has said a word. *You'd think Belzonia doesn't exist.*

"Can't put much faith in the rantin' of a buncha drunk niggers, Eli," Lennis told me in his in*finite* wisdom, "An' I'll tell you what else. If'n two northern white boys and a coupla northern coloreds came down here and got dealt a sour hand, well I say they got what they axed fer. No offense o' course."

"None taken, o' course."

I don't think anybody has worked it out that one of those white boys was me. The "unidentified white companion."

I've got a song in my head. Blind Willie Johnson. "God Moves on the Water. " I haven't heard that in years. I just realized I've been singing it to myself. Wonder how long I've been doing that?
" … *and de peopuh' come a-run and pray/ Lawd Lawd.*" Yeah! That's good shit! He wrote that song when the Titanic went under. Titanic. Tower of Babel. All the same to Blind Willie Johnson.

Reading over what Wolf said, I just can't work it out. Like what he said about Robert Johnson's death. I mean, the only person who "got Dusty" was whoever poisoned his drink. Whiskey and women. That's what killed Robert Johnson. He looked at some guy's chick too close, and the guy put him down. That's all there was to it, right?

Right?

Wolf is crazy. Paranoid. Just listen to the music he wrote! Or *is going to write.* All about folks trying to capture him, kill him, poison him, hunt him down ...

But it doesn't really happen.

?

Of course I'm the last person who should doubt anybody's story.

Something happened last night. Something *did* happen. Something. Was it really like I wrote it?

Lennis is watching me write this. I don't know why it puts him off so much.

"You writin' ever'thang down cuz yer a forgitful sumbitch, ain't that right?"

"You got it right, partner. Hey, Lennis? What do you know about a man named Walter Brown?"

Big thoughtful pause.

"Ain't never heard of 'im."

"Really? Colored man. Died a couple of years ago. Head injury."

Another big-ass pause.

"Hmm ... oh yeah. I 'member now. Worked Morton's farm a spell. Kinda uppity if'n I recall correctly. Thought he wuz Mr. Big-Stuff. Had a bee in his bonnet 'bout learnin' pickaninnies the two Rs. Now I can't figg'er what's the good o' readin' and writin' if'n you's gonna be down pickin' plants all day, but that wuz his mind. Some said he had an eye fer white women, but I don't think that wuz true. Truth be told, that nigger wuz a drunk, and he slipped in the mud down on the riverbank and cracked his noggin on a rocky patch. Too bad."

"Oh."

"Why you int'rested in alla that stuff?"

"Just ... tryin' to soak up some local color is all."

"Well … all right. You wantin' a lemonade?"
"Do chickens shit in the coop?"
"Yep. Reckon they do from time to time."

Hmmm.
Go figure.
Dinner time.

DEAREST ELI,

I hope everything is well with you. I heard from a couple of the gals that you ran into a bit of trouble in Belzoni a couple of nights ago. Now honey, I don't mean to sound like an old mother, even though that is what I am, but you should know better than to go into places like that. You just can't anticipate the savage behavior of some people.

On much happier business, Joe and I simply adore the portrait! You must come over and see it hanging so lovely in our dining room. I've told so many people about it, you will have more customers than you'll know what to do with! God bless you.

> Sincerely yours,
> Eddy McDaniel

DEAR DIARY,

It is Tuesday August the 23rd in the year of Our Lord 1938.

Don't rightly know why I writing this. Can't put to words what I be thinking. Thinking or feeling. Just funny thoughts in my head, Diary. Funny thoughts.

Just setting and wondering. Wondering what happens to a body's soul when the body shuts off. Ain't that somethin else? Such a thing to be thinking on.

Any old way, always figured every soul go off to Heaven. But I ain't so sure no more. Maybe, just maybe, some souls go somewheres else.

Now I don't mean no blasfemy, Lord. Just thinking is all. And I ain't talking no Hades neither. Good souls of good folks. Maybe if a body ain't took care of all they earthly business, then that soul got to come round to look after what gots to be done.

I can't reason all this. Probably just a plum loony. Ain't no counting for my pondering mind.

God bless Mae, and Mrs. Durning, and Charlie and Alberta, and Eli—even though he make me want to holler—and to all the souls of the dearly departed, if you all is hanging round here, why don't you say Hello.

AUGUST 23, 1938

Tomorrow I'm supposed to go see some lady about doing a portrait of her whole family. Mrs. Durning's friend. Mrs. Grand? Grant? Something like that. At any rate, she's got eight kids and somewhere in the vicinity of like twenty-nine grandkids. Must be "Papist." Man oh man what a job that's gonna be …

When I got home a bit ago, Ella was downstairs folding laundry. I came in and said, "Hey there."

"Hey there y'self," is what I got in reply. *Goddamn … did a cold breeze just shoot through here?* I know how this game goes. She'll try to give me the icy shoulder mixed with the silent treatment, but it won't last.

Sure enough …

"Of all the foolish … I swear to the good Lord above … If we goin' be friends, then you can't be … Lord give me strength … "

"Yeah, I know. I'm rotten. Mrs. Durning here?"

"Nuh, she visitin' with Mrs. Ross, and you's a lucky for that. You still lookin' beat ALL up. And Mrs. Grant and her husband expectin' you tomorrow mornin' for to start the picture paintin'. And Mrs. Conner wantin' you later—"

"I know all that, Ella. You've told me my schedule about seven times already."

"Well, if I's the only sensible round here … "

"You're too good to me, you know?"

"Haw, you can just keep that sugar for your tea, mister, cuz I ain't got no use for it."

Heh.

I knew she'd hidden a 78 of Roosevelt Sykes singing "The Honey Dripper" behind the pie chest in the kitchen. So I slipped out, grabbed it, and dropped it on the old Victrola. Ella bolts into the parlor all in a panic, and I'm getting my groove on like I do.

"You stop that, Eli! Where you find that? Quit being such a foolish!"

And Roosevelt is singing.

"Lookit here pretty mama, I really ain't got no home … "

"Your hiding spots are dismal," I told her, while I'm cuttin' a meeeean rug.

"Now, you goin' get us all in trouble!"

"I'm a dancin' machine, Ella Brown. Watchmegitdown."

"You's a crazy like a bug-house bat is what you is!"

And Roosevelt and I sang together, *"Will you let me drip my honey, baby, in your honeycomb?"*

"That there jus' scandalous … " she said.

"You bought it."

"Well, but see—"

"It's all right. Nobody's here, Ella dear."

"Mae be back directly from—"

"In an hour."

"Mrs. D goin' come back and it'll be curtains for sure!"

I'm workin' it. Workin' it! I cannot be stopped!

"Come on, Mrs. Brown. Give me this dance."

Sure, she tried to deny me … but NO woman can resist a man who moves like Groucho Marx on Angel Dust.

"Well … I reckon somebody got to give you a dance, cuz the one you gots is broke."

"I'm a bluesman, honey-chile. Bluesmen don't dance. Normally."

"Don't dance *normally*. Sure enough. And since when is you a *bluesman*?"

"Since forever. Howlin' Wolf calls me Red Devil Li."

"That there's the wuhst name I ever did hear."

Sing it, Roosevelt!

"Lord, I'll tell the world, that you is all right with me … "

"You gots all sorts of names, Mr. Tin-Pan-Alley."

"Well," I told her, taking it down for just a moment, "There was a girl back in the day who used to call me 'Li-la Delila.'"

"I done stand corrected. THAT'S the wuhst name I ever heard."

She laughed.

And I smiled.

And we *danced*.

Lord, I'll tell the world, that you is all right with me …

✹

K.

Watts in the sixties has always been a safe zone for me. *Not anymore.*

I rolled into town on August 11. It was 4:30PM and I found myself heading up Avalon Boulevard. I heard a car horn beep at me and I spun around and what do I find but two fool-grinning young brothers in a beat-down '55 Buick. "Well, well, well," I said, shaking my head, "The brothers Frye as I live and breathe."

"You know what I see in front of my eyes, Marquette?"

"What do you see, Ronald?"

"I see a poor lost sheep just a-yearnin' for salvation!"

"Haw preach 'em now."

"We must reach out to this wanderin' soul, my brother, Praise the Lord."

"Praise the Lord! But what, I ask, WHAT would soothe the tormented spirit of this rambling man?"

"Weeeell, I don't know of NO kinda hard driving what can't be made all right by some fine ladies and even finer liquor." And they both broke up laughing. "AMEN HALLELUJAH!"

"Y'all some cards." I said. "You should take this here act onna road."

"We is on the road, Blood!" Marquette announced. "Hop in."

"So Ronald," I asked as we drove a couple of blocks that we could have easily hoofed, "You still a fly bird for the U.S. nigger-killing machine?"

"No, brother Jerome, I am not. Discharged. So no Vietnam for me, uh uh. Course I ain't no more scared of Charlie than I am of Irvine." He's talking of white Cali cops, of course. Not the Irvine I know. *If he only knew ...*

The two young ladies at whose home we ended up were pretty enough. I didn't catch their names and I wasn't terribly interested. They were generous with their vodka, and that's all that occupied my mind just then. We sat and drank screwdrivers for a couple of hours, one of the girls trying really hard to "get to know me." *Good luck, lil mama.*

"I can just tell, you know," she slurred, "that you puttin' down a really heavy thing, Jerome. You know? And folks is always tellin' me that I gots intuition, and they can count on me, you know, so you don't got to be uptight about rappin' to me about, you know, any ole thang … " and so on and so on and so on.

"Right on, sista-lady," is all I said, downing another glass of liquid Russian death. Orange juice just gets in the way.

After a while it was time to head back to *la Casa de* Frye over at 11620 Towne Street. We bid the ladies farewell and stumbled back to the Buick. I knew Marquette wasn't right to drive, and some might say that if I had stopped him driving just then there wouldn't have been the fire and the beatings and explosions and death that followed. But I've been time walking long enough to know that that's a bunch of bullshit. So I didn't say a word.

We were just about two blocks from home when Officer *Okiefrommuskogee* pulled us over. Avalon and 116th. Everything was actually quite cool at first. We were clowning around with the cop and he was being a good sport. While running through the drunk-test questions, he asked Marquette what color his hair is (ignoring the fact that Marquette barely *has* any hair). "Black, sir," Marquette said trying not to laugh. "In fact I got black wrists and a black neck too." He rolled up his pants leg and pointed at his ankle. "In fact, I be pretty much *black all over.*"

Marquette utterly failed the sobriety test, but we still figured since no harm was done and we could easily walk home, that we'd be let go. Even when a crowd had started to gather and Marquette began performing and showing off for them I thought that all would end okay (though the officer was clearly starting to get nervous). But then we heard … *the voice.* Someone had run down and told Mama Frye that Marquette had been driving drunk and he's in trouble, and here she came marching up Avalon letting Marquette have it the whole way.

"Marquette! What kinda foolishness you up to here!?! You know DAMN well you ain't supposed to be drinking and driving! Just wait 'til your father git home and I tell him about this! You gonna be sorry you was born, damn it all! Hey, Jerome baby."

"Hey, Miz Rena," I said, sheepishly, also getting a bit nervous about my increasing profile right about then.

Marquette panicked at the sight of his mother. He'd had a long history of troubles: unemployment, in and out of jail, life generally had not gone well for him. But things being as they were, Mama was his tipping point. She grabbed his arm and he pushed her away. "I ain't drunk, Mama!" he screamed, and tried to run off. The cop then grabbed him, and Marquette *pushed him too.*

By this time little boy blue had called for backup and his nuts had been cut right off. The crowd had grown to about a hundred and folks had started taunting him. He decided that he *had* to arrest Marquette to get his nuts back … and so began the downward spiral into the fires of Hell.

Marquette had, by the time the second wave of officers arrived, taken to wandering through the crowd, cursing at random. Ronald and Mama had no luck calming him. These three new cops were no-nonsense from the get-go, their batons at the ready. As the crowd grew larger and taunts of "Whitey" and "blue-eyed devil" began to intensify, I tried to ease away from the scene. I didn't want to leave the Fryes high and dry, but self-preservation's a motherfucker, if you get my drift.

"I'm not going back to jail!" Marquette hollered, swinging sloppily at an officer. "You gonna have to kill me to take me to jail. I haven't did anything to be taken to jail!" At which point one of the cops punched him in the face and they cuffed him on the ground. As they threw Marquette in the back of the cruiser, one of them kicked him in the stomach and slammed his legs in the door.

"You ain't gotta do that!" someone yelled, and Rena jumped on the cop's back. The crowd began to surge angrily as more police arrived on the scene. A cop waved his shotgun indiscriminately, which sent a shock wave of panic coursing through the already agitated and ever-growing mob. Then one of those pigs punched Rena in the face and both Ronald and I lurched on him. I took a baton to the shoulder and fell to the ground, scraping my cheek against the asphalt. Looking up I saw Rena and Ronald both in handcuffs and some young woman with curlers in her hair from the beauty parlor across the street being dragged away by her neck.

"That girl's pregnant!" somebody yelled, "White devil's beating on that pregnant girl!" She didn't look pregnant to me, but by then it didn't matter. "They'd never treat a white woman like that!" Rage was brewing, and the crowd was growing massive. Some muffled megaphone voice told the officers to withdraw and they quickly fled the scene, the Fryes and beauty-shop girl in tow. A glass bottle went hurling toward the cruisers. Then another bottle. Then a chunk of sidewalk. Then a brick. Screaming, cursing, crying, the mob began to both gather and spread. "Goddamn them pigs!"

"Muthafuck the honkies!"

"Ain't gonna be NO REST for Whitey tonight!"

One man in the crowd I noticed was casually surveying the scene, an air of blank serenity about him. He turned to me ... and a smile like an ulcer with teeth ripped across his face. "Swing here, Kinnae," he hissed, twitching. And I tore off down Avalon.

❋

Dere Alberta

Hello Mimber me? This Mae McGhee we met sum time ago I wurk with Ella

I s sory if this aint a good leter I aint got much hand fo leter ritin like Ella do

My pupos fo ritin is that I think yous ot to cum en git Ella on cownt of I think she aint well

She bin havn spells of cryin an passin owt cold an up an down moods Rekon she weery from wurk but all so memry of Walter wont let her be an all so Lord fergiv me fo sayin but I think she doin sumthin that aint rite with a gest that stayin here a wite man You no I woodnt of thot of a thin like that if I wernt a hunert per cent fo sertin Plese cum soon I is sho wurryd bowt her an I dont no wut she likly to do

Sincerly

Willie Mae McGhee

August 25, 1938

God fucking damn it!! I can't find my journal anywhere. It's gotta be in this bedroom. I had it last night. I asked Ella if she'd seen it. She said "No," and I guess Mae wouldn't have messed with it because apparently she can't read. I keep it safe for just this reason, and now look! SHIT!!!!

I guess I'm just going to have to start a new one, but I really can't afford to have that fall into *anybody's* hands. *Anybody's.*

It's around here somewhere. Just gotta keep looking.

❋

DEAR DIARY,
It is August the 26th in the year of Our Lord 1938.
Oh Lordy Lord! This going to sound like such a foolish—not even foolish but just a down right crazy, but I reckon I finally can reason everything! I done figured it all out. The whole confusing mess. Now bear with me, Diary, cause I told you it was—

DEAR LENNIS,

It is with a heavy heart that I write this. I have read through the "journal" that you gave me to read, and I must say it is the most troubling thing to pass my way in some time. I know that you and your good wife Anna have grown quite attached to this Eli Cooper, and I certainly understand. On the two or three occasions I had to speak with him, I found him to be both charming and spirited. On the other hand, Lennis, he is clearly not of sound mind, and I believe that he is a danger to himself and to our community.

Within this journal of his, he makes repeated mention of killing himself and other people. He appears to delight in being a thief and a liar. He is obsessed with this fantasy that he is from the future. He admits to having lustful thoughts regarding Gladys Durning's colored girl, and quite frankly, I can't recall in my life ever reading so much blasphemy, vulgarity, obscenity, and profanity on the written page.

As much as it pains me to say so, I think we should seriously consider having your friend put away. For his safety as well as for ours. He will get the treatment he needs. I truly feel that this is for the best.

Yours in Christ,
Rev. Thomas Fisher

August 26, 1938

goddamn
motherfucking
monsters

Two men, two Black men, have just been found dead in the woods. Lynched. *Fucking lynched.*

What kind of sick, twisted, depraved psychopath could set another human being on fire??!
ON FIRE!!!!

Probably a psychopath I say good morning to every day. Could be fucking anybody. Could be fucking all of them. MURDERING BASTARDS!!!!

I gotta go there. I gotta see. Something's telling me I have to go.

I just wanna see the streets of downtown lined with dead white bodies. *Hang them by their fucking guts.*
As white as death itself.

What do I say to Ella? She won't stop crying. She and Mae are in the living room sobbing their eyes out.

"There, there, sweeties," says Mrs. Durning. "There there. This business … It's just unpleasant, to be certain."

Yeah yeah, Mrs. D. Ignore the horror. It's not really there.

None of the other men will leave their rooms. Guilty conscience, boys?
This is Hell. This is Hell. This is Hell. This is Hell. This is Hell. *This is Hell.*

What can I say to her? I want to hold her so bad … say something. Say nothing. Just be there. And I can't. I can't. Look at me! White as death itself.

Ella and Mae knew one of the men. The one that was burned alive. I haven't caught his name.

Nobody knows who the other man was. Guess he was from out of town. Hanged.

Must have done something unthinkable like keep his head up.

✳

DEAR DIARY,

I cannot live like this no longer! I cannot. Every time this happen I dies a little. Fore too long I be dead as all the rest.

Lord All Mighty in Heaven please forgive me for saying this, but I just wanting to see the streets downtown lined with dead white bodies!

I cannot be trapped in this no longer

I gots to get away to somewhere anywhere

Mae run in screaming and crying ELLA YOU GOTS TO COME QUICK!

What is it child? I ask. But I ain't got to ask. I knows. I knows it like my own name God Almighty.

Mae, bless her heart, she try so hard.

But I ain't got nothing left. Nothing left Lord.

Lessee now, she say after a good while of weeping and crying, I reckon every body done been alerted by now. We all going be at the Tilsons' first thing in the morning, Ella. Poor Mabel and the childrens. You and me can fix up some cornbread, Ella, and Pastor Johnson—

And she say some more stuff. But I can't hear her none. It's a tragic. Sure enough is.

Mae she stamping her little feet—

Ella Brown you gots to stop all this mess now!

But I be trapped in a moment, yessir.

Mabel gonna need us all to be strong for her, Ella! For the babies. That's how we going have healing.

Healing? Healing.

I tells her I don't give two bits for no healing Mae. Not two damn bits. Some wounds don't never heal Mae. They best not to. So I don't care none for no goddamn healing.

Ella! Stop it now! She say crying. You scaring me!

Well I scares me too Mae. And I ain't studying on no more healing. I be fixing to study on bloodletting instead.

Forgive me, Lord.

O and don't you know Mrs. D she come in right then talking bout There there, sweeties. This business is just unpleasant, to be certain.

God in Heaven give me strength.

O yes sir and she saying she know we upset now

but it will pass.

Mrs. D, I don't want it to pass! I don't want nothing to be okay never! They set poor Reggie Tilson ON FIRE! Reggie gots a wife and seven childrens and now they ain't nothing! They ain't got nothing! Nothing but DEATH!

And all she could say was

Reggie was a real nice boy.

He was a MAN.

Lord give me strength, he was a man.

✻

AUGUST 27, 1938

It wasn't really a long walk. Or maybe it was. I just kind of shifted into automatic. Some Black children had discovered the bodies. And the bodies stayed there for a good long while. There was a walking caravan of white folk headed that way, so I just blended in. The whole vibe was very matter-of-fact. People weren't crude or disrespectful in any specific way. Just kind of chit-chatting about this or that. Like we were heading to a swap meet or a flea market or a church picnic. By the time we got there, there was a bit of a crowd already assembled. Just kind of chit-chatting away about this or that ... while sheriff Hank Ross and one of his deputies cut the first man down.

Yeah, it was *him*. That guy from Morton's farm on the 8th. I'd never seen a dead body in public before, and I almost feel like I still haven't. He looked like a painted mannequin. Not really brown any more. Almost purple. Well dressed in a real all-purpose kind of way. Looked like foam and rubber. But he's real. And he's dead. And he was murdered. And people just chit-chatted away. And this little red-headed girl looked at him just real bland and content.

This is hell.

I almost didn't notice the other man. Reggie Tilson. Reggie Tilson husband of Mabel Tilson son of Fannie and Mose Tilson. Father of seven little Tilsons. I almost didn't notice him tied by the wrists around the trunk of the poplar. The left side of his body so scorched and burned away he was fused to the bark. One with the tree. Burned together. The right side of his body so perfect he looked almost alive in profile. And folks just chatted. What, no one brought the lemonade and pie? There's a burned up corpse tied to a tree trunk. Somebody strike up the band!

Papers scattered all about the ground. Burned beyond comprehension. People just walking through them. I try to gather a few up, but nothing's legible. One page, very top, reads: *The Time Walker's Blu* and then just charred black.

I had to step away. Walked a piece into the woods. I saw that little Black boy. Lafeyette's his name? I'm almost positive.

"Strange fruit, suh. Scary sho' enough, but I ain' scared none."

"I am."

"If you please, suh, I needs a message give to Miss Ella Brown. Tell her I says … I sees her man."

"That's not possible," I said.

But he was gone.

Sheriff Hank Ross and his deputy rifled through the hanged man's jacket. Then they both looked right at me. Then everyone looked right at me. He held an envelope that he pulled out of the dead man's shirt pocket. And he walked over and handed it to me, and it read:

ELI COOPER

To: Mr. Eli Cooper c/o the James Durning Estate
PRIVATE

Dear Eli,

Hello. Let me get straight to the point. I've come to bring you home. That's right. I'm come to take you back from the land-that-time-forgot. I've found the way to go back and forth with ease. It's really quite simple. You'll see.

You really have settled in nicely around here. Really pulled a fast one on these 'seeds, eh? Good for you, my boy. I also know that you've found someone you don't want to leave behind. Not a problem. You convince her to tag along, and she can come at no extra cost to you. Just a little bonus because that's the kind of guy I am. That reminds me: I'm afraid I'm going to have to ask for a modest service fee. I know you don't have much, monetarily speaking, but once we are back in civilization again, I understand you will be worth a sizable amount. Especially now—rising from "the grave" and all.

So get your lungs prepared for the smog, get your attitude in shape for the crowds, and get your heart set on the Apple, cuz we are going home!

I will be by to meet you in two days (August 29) late evening. The night time is the right time! By morning, you and I—or the three of us (or maybe even the FOUR of us)—will be having breakfast in Chinatown. Stay cool 'til then.

Sincerely,
Jerome Kinnae

August 29, 1938

This is the song in my head:

Keep yo' lamp trimmed and burnin'/ see what yo' God has done/ Brotha don't get worried/ cuz the work is 'most done ...

I was at the Martins'. Real quiet there. Lennis didn't know what to say to me, and Anna kept acting like nothing was wrong. Sheriff Ross stopped by. He and Anna and Lennis have known each other since they were children. It was a *friendly call.* I don't know why, but somehow I ended up laid out on the floor.

Hank started asking me about "Jerome Kinnae," the words "nigger got what he deserved" were spoken, I called him a "pig," and he jacked me right in the eye. Anna screamed at him to GIT OUT!!! So he did. And Lennis didn't say anything.

"Aw Eli, darlin', are you okay?" she asked. I nodded and just stumbled out the door. "No, don't go, honey! Yer gonna git a black eye if we don't—"

"I already do," I said, but I was so addled from the punch my voice sounded funny. Last thing I heard as I left the house was Lennis shouting, "Let'm go, Anna."

Back home. Mrs. Durning has asked me to leave. Move out. No job. Pariah.

"Very sorreh, dea'. Very sorreh."

❀

L.

At the corner of Avalon and Imperial Highway people were pelting a passing bus with chunks of wood and scrap iron. Traffic screeched to a halt as the mob waded into Imperial. A wail of sirens started up in the distance, and more and more answered its cry. As I watched a middle-aged white man being dragged out of his car, I headed back up to 116th Street, my eyes scanning for *Them* at every turn. (*They*'re on the scene. *They*'re hunting for me.) A quick left on 116th toward Central Avenue and I saw the first of what would be many cars burst into flames.

There's a path at Athens Park, I thought, running full speed north on Avalon toward El Segundo. I couldn't remember where it leads, but fuck it. "Whitey's gonna pay!" someone screamed. "This be for Joyce Ann!" Whoever that is.

The jig was up at 120th Street. Five pigs on motorcycles screeched in, forming a circle around me. Pinned on all sides. There are few feelings worse than being tangled up in blue … and this was much worse. Once they had me surrounded they dismounted … and *continued circling.* "I just want to get home, officers," I said holding up my hands where they could see them. To which they all removed their helmets at the same time … the moment dropped to a hush … all of *Their* white faces grinning, all *Their* dead blue eyes fixed on me.

"*Home,* Jerome?" one said. "Now, all of us here know you've *got no home.* So where you gonna run to, boy? You know you can't hide. I'd say you should just come with us, but you know by now where *that's* leading, right?"

"Swing here, boy … " *They* hissed. "Swing here … "

"Can't never hide … "

"You know," I said, swallowing all the terror I could, "Those are some pretty fine new uniforms y'all have. Looks like they've never seen any action at all."

"They will … "

"Y'all gotta be trippin' thinkin' you're gonna come at me *tonight* dressed like honky pigs. No fear. I got no fear."

"You will … "

Got to think. Got to plan. I've weaseled my way out of this before.

"Finish … you … "

One of *Them* doubled over gurgling and grasping his throat. He convulsed as ribbons of blood began to spill through his fingers onto the asphalt, a sickening hoarse bark retching out of him. "Now look what you've done," another said to me, chuckling. The rest of *Them* twitched as *They* advanced on me, hunching like twisted mantes.

A building which must have been on or near Compton Avenue exploded in fire. A mob came charging up 120th from Willowbrook. "Ain't gonna be no rest for Whitey tonight," I whispered to *Them* and turned toward the advancing mob. "Willowbrook!" I shouted, throwing up three fingers. "Blood brother! OFF THE PIGS!!!" Within seconds the mob came crashing down on *Them* like a tidal wave on a sand castle. And I darted off toward Broadway. *If I can get there it's left on Broadway and 120th.* One block to Athens Park. *If only …*

I made it as far as San Pedro Street. Crowds were thick there and the gunfire had started up. Someone had shot out the streetlights. Explosions in the distance. They almost seemed systematic, and I found myself counting the minutes between them, as if anticipating thunder crashes. (As the hours advanced those minutes would become seconds, and the sound of shooting guns would just meld with the atmosphere like country cricket bows.) An abandoned apartment building on San Pedro and 120th seemed like an ideal spot to hide out … which proves just how wrong my instincts can be sometimes.

✻

AUGUST 29
Really fucked up now. Not even sure what happened exactly.
Ella came into my room. I didn't even realize, but my nose was bleeding.
"You bleeding! You hurt!"
"No, I'm okay. When I'm upset, blood leaks from my head. Always has. Weird, huh."
"I reckon. You ain't got no more picture paintin' jobs."
"I know."
"That Rev'rend Fisher been tellin' folk you out to be locked up. Folks thinkin' you's a crazy."
"I reckon."
"I knows just how that be. Seem everything goin' to Hades. I went to church with one of them what they found ... Reggie ... the other one, nobody know ... Nobody know ... "
"Ella, I'm so, so sorry to hear about Mr. Tilson."
She just shrugged, and kinda laughed a little.
"Bein' colored in Mississippi like some sort of punishment. But I don't reckon it's no better nowheres else. It happen all the time ... but ... don't never get use to it. Can't nev' scrub it offa ya. It jus' make a body cold an' bitter when you realize that your life ain't worth nothin' to nobody."
I can ... only imagine.
"I shouldn't even tell you this," she said. "And Lord forgive me for even repeatin' it. But years ago my Walter's good friend done got *lynched*. White lady said he got fresh, or some nonsense. Walter such a angry he scream right inna middle of town one day. He done screamed, 'Sometimes I just wanna see the streets of this town lined ... ' Oh Lord forgive him. He ain' mean it. Just so upset. They done killed so ... It weren't long after that he done had his little ole 'accident.'"
"What did he say?"
"He ain' mean it! Just a furious—"
"What did he say?"
"He say, 'I just wanna see the streets of this town lined with—'"
"Dead white bodies," we said together.

Startled both of us.

"How you ... ?"

"I don't know."

I don't know.

"The night they come told me about Walter ... It weren't no accident! Yous murdered him! Yous MURDERED HIM! I wanna see dead WHITE bodies! DEAD WHITE BODIES! I was ... Got a mind to run run run ... Far away ... but I reckon it ain't no better nowheres else."

"They trade the rope and the torch for bullets and Drug Wars," I said. "But it's the same ole lynch mob."

Same ole lynch mob ...

"I went and saw them, Ella. There was a little boy there and he told me to tell you—"

"Please don't say!!!" She cried, and covered her ears. Doubled over, clutching her stomach. Rocking back and forth.

None of my business.

"Okay. Okay ... "

I asked her if I could put my arms around her.

And she didn't answer me for a thousand years ... but then she said,

"I reckon."

So I did. Could have held her forever. Forever. Forever. *Gonna trap me in a moment? Trap me in this one.*

"I am never gonna let you get away again," I whispered. She looked at me. Puzzled.

"What you mean?"

How could I say it?

"Nothing," I said. "I have something for you."

From under the bed, I pulled out my sketchbook and two canvases. I showed her the portrait of her dancing in the parlor.

"For you. It IS you. As you can ... see."

"It's a ... breathtakin'," she whispered, "I don't got words for it. You done made me a more beautiful than I really is."

"I could never paint you as *the beautiful* you really are."

Are we really doing this?

"This is a nice too," she said, pointing at the *brownstone.*
"If you like it, you can have it. It's a pretty good likeness, but not exactly what I'd hoped for."
    She pointed to the *Jessie* in my sketchbook and arched her eyebrow.
    "And who that?"
Oh ...
    "That's ... that's ... that is ... that there ... be my wife. *My little bitty pretty one.*"
That's what I said. But—
I
don't
sound
like
me
anymore

M.

The joint was filthy, decrepit and dark. I headed straight for the roof to catch a proper panorama. There I watched my beloved Watts burning. I could just barely make out the Army surplus store on Avalon being emptied out. Then it went up in flames. Loot, burn. Loot, burn. Like it was *planned*. Over the next few days the rioting would take on a sophisticated level of organization. LAPD and the California Highway Patrol would be deliberately diverted from a scene with misleading phone reports; then a wave of people would charge in and loot. A second group would then burn the store down. When firefighters arrived they'd be attacked by debris and sniper fire. Black shopkeepers would hang signs in the window, "This is a Negro-owned Business," "Blood Brother," and they'd be spared. At first. White cops were the primary targets, though whites in general were marked. "Negro-friendly" white businesses would be spared. At first. Bullets flew from rooftops throughout town, but no one was killed. At first. But by Friday the thirteenth madness would take over, as madness is wont to do. And until Friday all of this gathering chaos was nothing but a soundtrack to me.

I sat on that rooftop for hours watching the show. *Grotesque burlesque*, I thought. *Flaming psychotic Vaudeville.* Where righteous payback meets naked opportunism by way of blood-mad insanity. *Works for me.* Billowing black smoke blotted out most of the stars. But for a brief moment I thought for sure I saw a meteorite shoot through the sky.

Watts, Compton, Willowbrook, whites have long called this side of LA "Mudtown." I've always considered it a good place to call 'home' for short spells.

"But you've got no home," a voice said from behind, and frozen horror shot right through me. *I could maybe survive a six floor jump,* I thought. *But I won't be able to run.* So I sat still. He didn't growl or whoop or screech, he didn't hiss or twitch. He just walked over and sat down on the corner of what must have once been a chimney top. I looked over at him and his throat was fine. And he wasn't particularly well dressed. He just looked … *average.*

"Did you hear," he continued, "somebody shot Dick Gregory in the thigh? Oh wait … that hasn't happened yet."

"So what can I do for ya, *officer?*" *Could I really sit and have a conversation with one of Them? Could stranger things happen?*

"Just got a question, Jerome. When's it gonna end, huh? Is this really how you're going to spend the rest of your forever? No past, no purpose, no hopes or dreams, no identity, no family, no *self*, just rampaging through time causing chaos and disorder?"

"I'm not a fucking rampager."

"Are you serious?" He laughed, indicating the burning landscape. "What do you call *this*?"

"This isn't my fault."

"Yeah. Just what every rampager says."

"Uh huh … so if I hadn't come here, then Ronald and Marquette would have stayed the night with those two girls, right? They never would have been pulled over, and Watts would not have gone up in flames. Is that what you're saying? Is that my crime? Then go back and settle me before it happens."

"This is what happens now. What's done is done. It's a larger pattern of disruption that you're causing, kid. You've tangled yourself up in a far stickier moment than this."

"Hell with that. I don't believe in time loops, or pockets, or trapped moments. Delusion and ignorance all of it."

"Well, you're certainly trapped in this one. What's your name, Jerome?"

"Jerome Kinnae."

"What's your fucking name … " he hissed. Eye twitched. I looked back at the door to downstairs. *Never make it.* "What's your name, Jerome?"

"I don't know."

"Jump. Settle this. You've caused enough damage."

"What's YOUR fucking name?"

"You've got two options, ole son. Remain nameless and hunted, trapped in time, or do us both and the world a favor and *die right now.*"

"Two options … "

"Sure, there is a third, but trust me, you don't want to take that route."

"What if *you* jumped?"

"Maybe I can't. Maybe it wouldn't make any difference."

"Maybe that's just more lies and manipulation."

"We don't manipulate, dog. We *destroy* manipulators."

"You've got to know that I don't much care for white people. Dog. So why are you coming dressed like a peckerwood? I'm not scared of them. And if persuasion or seduction are your game, then coming as a fine sista would have done you way more good." He just laughed. And then he started *singing*.

"I'm gonna lay/ lay my head/ on some loooooooonesome railroad line/ and let the 219 train pacify my mind."

"I've heard that before … "

"Your time is running out, Jerome. You're getting more careless and cocky all the time. You're walking into the spider web. The noose is tightening around your neck. Make it easy on yourself."

I stood up and peered over the side of the roof. Then I looked back at him. *He's just a man like me,* I thought. Then I grabbed him by his hair and slammed his throat into the corner of the old brick chimney. He fell to the floor screeching and gurgling, thrashing and twitching like a dying crane. I yanked off a heavy chunk of the crumbling chimney and brought it down, crushing his rib cage. He shrieked and shot out a fist, curled like a talon, toward my face. I darted off down the steps. Floor after floor I could hear him whooping and scurrying, galloping, sounding less human by the moment. Just as I reached the ground floor I saw him whip past the front door. Then whip back before it again. He gathered at the bottom of the stairs and paused. Glared right at me. Time locked shut. Blood and teeth and convulsing rage twisting he lunged toward me and I tore up to the next floor and into the darkness. Into an apartment … windows boarded shut. I could hear him barreling up and down the corridor, gurgling and retching something that sounded like "Pit for you." Over and over, "Pit for you." *Pit for you. Pit for you. Pit for you.* And so it went. I'd hear him gallop to a different floor, and I would leave my place and try to escape. He would come after me and I would hide. A closet. A storage room. Another apartment, boarded windows. More gurgling, snarling, shrieking. *Pit for you, pit for you, pit for you.*

✳

ELLA GASPED and covered her face and ran out of the room crying.
FUCK.

Mrs. Durning came storming in.

"Mistah Coopah, I am sorreh but you simpleh'must leave mah house. I cannot allow this kind of behaviah. Now I don't know what it is you've done, but you know as well as I do that talking in a hu'tful fashion to simple people is just not propah. You have made po' little Ella cry. That is not propah."

Simple ...

"Ah's sho' sorry Mrs. D. We wuz jes' talkin' is all. Ain't mean no hahm."

That's what I said.

That's what I sounded like.

It is another man another man's voice I swear to fucking god.

Mrs. Durning was not amused.

"Mistah Coopah, I recommend that you spend a little mo' time with yo' own kahnd and a little less time both'ring mah maids. Talk is all ovah town about you, and I simpleh cannot allow you to bring any mo' shame to this house."

"Whut you reck'n Ah do?" I asked.

Who the fuck is that?!?!

"You may not eat suppah heah tonight. You may not sleep heah. I want you gone by mo'ning fuhst thing."

I will be long gone by morning. Don't you worry none.

❋

DEAR DIARY,

He done proved it! I can't reason how it could be, but what I spected is true!

He come back for me. He come back for me! Hallelujah Praise Jesus he done proved it!

But why he come back a white man? No telling. God, why a white man? For to protect him this time? The Lord he work in misterious ways.

After I run from the room, I heard Mrs. D give him seven shades of grief. I just wanting to holler He My Husband! But that would be a crazy.

So I waited. Waited. Crying my fool eyes raw. Then I crep up the stairs again, and I could hear my baby singing. Sing them songs. Just like it was.

I couldn't wait no longer! I run into the room crying,

I know you come back for me! I know you done it! Say who I am again, I says to him. Say it once more.

He say, You—my—little bitty pretty one?

And you my little school boy!

I just throw my arms round him and I kiss him and kiss him and then I kiss him some more! I could feel them tears running down my cheeks. You come back for me? I be weeping, You come back for me, baby?

I come back for you, he say. I loves you, Ella Brown. I loves you more than anything.

Don't never leave me again, I was at the sobbing by now, Don't never again!

I won't, he say. I won't never again. But will you come with me if I go?

I will. Lord yes I will.

Just then Mrs. D hurry in saying, There be none of that indecentness in this house! Mr. Cooper you get out now!

But he my husband! I hollered at her. She run out just a confused. I can't rightly blame her. I be one as well.

Get out now Mr. Cooper! Mrs. D scream from the hallway, Get out of my house or I will have to fetch the police!

My baby turn to me and he say, Now listen. I going go into town for to keep some peace round here. Can't stay. You pack up whatever you needs. We leaving tonight if that pleasing you.

Course it is, I say. I loves you!

I loves you, he say.

And he just left.

Lord God in Heaven Most High, thank you for what you done give to me! More than I could ever dream!

August 29, 1938
She knows.

Crazy business. Don't know why or how …
But goddamn it, she is my wife! I kissed her. That's the thing.
You know your wife's kiss. That's *it*.

We are together again! Why like this? Why here? Why *back*
here. I can't never get from back here. Wolf said it. Mississippi got
that hard pull.

Little concerned about my present situation. *Why the hell did
I come to this joint?* Sitting in Charlie's Place trying to get a cheese
sandwich and a lemon Coke. I shouldn't have come here. Every time
I speak, it's that *voice*. And it don't match. It don't match the face. I
catch my reflection in the glass, and Eli Cooper come staring back
at me. Who else do I expect?

I ain't going to understand any of this.

*Just get me through this night. I do not care where we are tomor-
row. Just as long as we are together.*

Nobody will wait on me. People all around are whispering. As
if I can't hear them.

"That ther's the one the Rev'rend talked about."
"Why don't he knock at the back door? We always throw food
to 'em."
"Didn't he see the sign 'White dining'?"
"I didn't know trees in these parts growed white fruit."

I keep checking my reflection in the glass, and Eli Cooper keeps
on staring back at me.
Who else do I expect?
Here comes Lennis. Wonder what he's wanting.

✳

N.

The sun rose Thursday morning I'm sure, but I didn't see it. I sat perfectly still, awake and exhausted, wondering if it was too late to swan dive off the roof. Wondering about the *third* option. There was brief respite outside, and then the gunshots, the sirens, and explosions started up again. I've heard there was a full moon Thursday night. Well I'll be damned.

I came to hunker down in a third floor apartment the morning of the thirteenth when I heard a rustle in the closet. "Please help me," a voice whimpered from inside. I thought for a moment that it might be him laying a trap for me, but then I heard him gallop, shrieking down the corridor below. *Could be another one of Them,* I thought, but I opened the door anyway. Curled up in the back of the closet was a woman, maybe late thirties, early forties.

"What's your name, sister?" I asked.

"Rita," she sniffled. "What is that *thing*?"

"Don't worry. He's not here for you."

We sat there most of the afternoon with no better plan than *make-a-break-for-it.* And as the day labored on, the violence outside raged harder than ever.

"'Fore I come to hide out here," Rita said. "I seen them boys pull a bunch of white folk out they cars and beat 'em real bad. Right there inna middle of the street."

"How did that make you feel?"

"I ain't feel nothing."

And, of course, more of *Them* came. The whoops and screeching echoed throughout the building. Accompanied occasionally … by soft, muffled music. And although my frazzled nerves and sleep deprivation may have led my ears astray, I swear I heard *bland, banal conversation* in the halls. I couldn't make out words, just the unmistakable sound of useless chatter. Rita heard it too. I told her that *They* wouldn't touch her and she should just run, but she would not listen. We watched twilight seep in through a crack in a window board, and outside someone yelled, "Burn, baby! Burn!" A crash was heard downstairs and all went silent. We ventured out to the hallway to find the first floor at the bottom of the stairs burning. Another cocktail flew through the door splashing fire up the walls. We had no choice. I grabbed Rita's hand and we dashed down the steps. Piercing shrieks came from all sides as we ran straight through the fire. I heard Rita scream, "Oh my god what ARE THEY?!?!" but I did not look, I just barreled forward out the door. A cocktail sailed past my head and crashed behind me as we breached the front entrance. I heard Rita wail and I turned my head to see her engulfed in flame. She pulled free of my grip and ran screaming down 120th—the fire burning her worse as she ran. "RITA! FALL TO THE GROUND!!!!" I hollered running after her, desperate for a ripple or an extra moment of time to catch her. But there was nothing. And there was nothing I could do. She hit the pavement dead and burning right in front of me. And there was nothing I could do. The building full of *Them* blazing behind me, and I'd have been just fine with them running out to finish me right then and there. But they didn't. And there was nothing I could do.

❈

Shit! Gotta catch my breath! Just ran four blocks.

Lennis came up to the counter and sat next to me.

"Won't serve ya will they," he said. "Let me try an' git somethin' for ya."

"Ah don' need your charity, friend-boy. You looking at a man right here."

"Jesus! Yer even startin' to talk like a nigger! Eli. Talk serious to me. I am yer friend. I know you got some sorta ... feelings for that colored girl, an' I want you to know that it's okay. It surely is okay. We don't punish our own fer that sorta thang. We don't hurt our own. It's okay. Been goin' on fer as long as them niggers been round here. Why, even back on the old ships, they used to use the females just to cap off the night."

I punched him in his goddamn throat and hollered at the top of my lungs:

"You talking 'bout my wife like that, cracker? Ah got a mind to kill you! Ah am gonna remember all you sorry fuckers WHO AH AM!"

Thanks, Wolf.

I ran out the door and darted up the street. Saw the crowd spill out of Charlie's like a swarm of angry hornets.

But then, all at once, they stopped. Stopped cold. And real slow like moseyed back to the cafe.

And here I am. On this here bench. Get it all down for posterity.

There—

Something's coming out of—
toward me.
it's him
one of *Them*

❉

O.

I lumbered down 120th like the risen dead. As far as I could see whole blocks were coated in flame. Sirens whined, guns popped as snipers shot wildly with no discernible target in mind. Police cruisers were set back to front as makeshift barricades, the LAPD picked off marauders left and right. Gunning them down like rabid animals. And I simply walked through it all. Looking through broken-out shop windows, 'customers' casually picked out goods. Then once they were satisfied with their haul and the shelves were cleared, they would wander away, and the building would be burned to the ground. A sign lay flat in the street which read, "Turn Left Or Get Shot," which was probably fine advice in its standing form.

At 120th and Central Avenue, the Shoprite Food Market fire raged. The firefighters watched it crumble and burn, powerless to stop it. For a moment one of them looked at me, and I was sure he was my rooftop *Dog,* but in a moment he was gone and he may have never been there at all.

"Hey!" some girl hollered to me. "Wasn't you with Marquette Frye when they took him away?"

"What, am I fucking Saint Peter up in here?" I asked. "How many times has the cock crowed?"

"Fuck you. It was just a question."

"Fuck you for asking." *Athens Park,* I thought. *Where is Athens Park?* And I turned back just in time to see a billy-club flying at my forehead.

✳

I'M DOWN ON THE ROAD BY THE DURNING ESTATE. Sheriff talking to Mrs. D. No mystery what they're talking about. I'll just hide out here till he leaves. Everything going be okay so long as I can get to Ella before THEY get here.

After everybody done went *oozing* on back into Charlie's Place, that "slick nigguh" from Harlem Tavern came sauntering out of the darkness. Smiling *that smile.* Carrying a glass of what looked like soda. I ain't running.

"Say there, my good man. Look what I brought you. A lemon Coke. Now I know you want it. I know you're dying for a drink. Go ahead, kid."

Took a drink. Drank it down. Had to.

"There's a good boy."

"So what you wanting with me, huh?"

"Ha ha ha! Finally sounding yourself again! That's mighty fine! I just wanna ask a coupla questions, friend-boy. For one, how you know this is all really happening? What if you just went bananas back in your 'old life.' Huh? What if you're there in New York right now, sitting in some alley drooling on yourself. Fantasizing you got your dead wife back. Fantasizing you're kickin' it in the Delta with Howlin' Wolf. Your friends been looking for you all this time and there you are all covered in piss on Bowery. Your nose is bleeding, son. Maybe somebody is kicking you in your face."

"When Ah get upset, blood leaks from my head."

"Don't I know it, kid. Don't I know it."

"Who is you, huh? Who is you, *friend-boy*?"

"Does it bother you to see me like this, huh? Dressed in your race? Would you prefer if we had glowing red eyes, claws, and sharp teeth, biting at your ankles? As you attempt escape after futile escape? Cuz we can work it that way too, boy. Ask poor ole Robert Johnson. Any way that will settle you the quickest and most thorough. We're getting a mite sick of you, quite frankly. How 'bout if we come in the middle of the night and knock at your door. You sprinkle all the hot juju powder you want, we'll still keep knocking.

All night long. Scratch at your window. Whisper your name in the dark 'til you just go crazy. Paranoid. Like the Wolf."

"You don't never catch the Wolf. You fail."

"Oh gracious. You are not hearing me, son. Don't you get it? Time keeps on playing! Over and over. This ain't a one-shot. We'll get him. Don't you worry 'bout that. We will settle the Wolf, just like we settle everybody who steps out of time. Out of line. Out of order. Now don't be cross. We're just keeping things tidy. It's our job. *Somebody has to maintain order.* If *We* don't, why then everything and everybody could be trapped forever in one moment. Just like you, friend-boy. And that wouldn't do, now would it?"

"Just go on with your talk, monkey-ass. Just go on."

"So you're signifying now, huh? Such rage. *Tsk tsk.* It's just unpleasant, to be certain. How 'bout if we come dressed in white sheets and pointed hoods? How would that suit ya, boy? Would that fix your little red wagon? I'll never forget the last time they done you. You looked up, eyes smashed and bloodshot, nose and mouth streaming blood, and you said to them—"

"This moment ... don't never forget it ... "

"Goddamn! Now that was beautiful, Brown! Absolutely beautiful. I believe they never did forget it. Somewhere shallow in their pathetic, feeble, retarded little minds, they watch you die forever. They watch you die out the corner of their eyes. Forever and ever. But you thought you were slick hiding out in another man's skin. White skin no less."

"Eli Cooper ... "

"Whatever you say. How could you know you'd play it out again yourself over and over."

"When Ah get upset—"

"Blood leaks from your head. I know. I know. You're trapped, Brown. You're all trapped. Trapped forever in this moment. We've seen all this before, you see? The one thing we didn't anticipate was your bitch—sorry. Your woman. Sweet Jesus! Never thought she'd break through! Never thought we'd have to settle her, but looks like we might after all. She chased you too, right? Can't have her running all over the place, now can we? Gotta keep order. Reign in the chaos. Time is all fouled up but we will settle it right again. We will settle her."

"NO!"

"That's right, friend-boy."

I try to scream that she ain't never done nothing and leave her alone but I couldn't make no sound. It ain't me. I ain't me.

"Just so you know," he said, *and he don't look right*, "I already know how this is going to play out. You are too late. Always too late. Two hours too always too late, ha! Those pigs in white sheets will intercept you and bash you to death, Brown. Just like they did last time, Brown. Only this time, Brown, SHE will see it happen. And she will run screaming into the night. And we will settle her. Just like the Wolf … we will settle her." Twisted up like a bird. Shaking. Twitching. Shrieking—"Whoo well well. We'll settle her."

I ran. Gonna grab her and we'll be gone as soon as I can—
Oh Jesus thank God that cop finally leaving!
wait
there's hollering
who is hollering?
Headlights up the road
It—

.

PART FIVE

LONELY ONE IN THIS TOWN

How long, how long, has that ev'nin' train been gone? How long?
How long, baby, how long?
—LEROY CARR

To: coopjdli@earthlink.net
From: serjnamie@yahoo.com
Sent: 7/5/01
Subject: jessie's dance

Wuzzup, Li-dog? Just making sure your single-minded ass remembers what night tonight is.
The time: 9:00 in the PM. The place: Burroughs. The star: You know her best. B–there, C–ya then. Oh yeah! Howz the jacket piece coming? Grapevine says it looks like Bacon. Don't sweat, you're still legit.
Serj
❈

P.

And so I woke up in the joint. Maybe this isn't Lincoln Heights Jail. I'm not sure. I don't really care. My head is throbbing. I barely remember getting processed. But I am grateful for the time-out.

Amir is sketching and singing to himself. This is what he's singing:

"I got the key to the highway/ Billed out and bound to go/ I'm gonna leave here running/ Walking is most too slow ... "

I've decided that that would be a fine title for this thing I'm writing here, so I've gone back to the first page and added it.

"Whose song is that?" I asked.

"Big Bill Broonzy," the white boy answered. "Good stuff."

"I don't know where," Amir said to me, "but I seen you before."

"I've been time walking for quite a while," I replied.

"Time walking. That's a serviceable enough name for it." Amir said. "I ain't done it for twenty-seven years and I don't plan to ever again."

"This is only my second walk, as you call it," the white boy said. "There's a trail from Athens Park that'll lead here from Sacramento 2004."

"I wasn't aware of that one," I said. "So how's it feel to be the only white in a jailhouse full of brothers?"

The boy just shrugged. "That's how I roll. This isn't the first California jail I've been in, honestly. First in '65, though. So, fuckin' ... here's to new experiences and shit. I found the, I don't know ... what would you call it ... the trail here, I found it by accident one night high as hell. Thought I must have hallucinated it. Sojourned on back just to see. I came here specifically because I've always been curious about the Riot."

I had to laugh. You can always spot a novice when they refer to their present situation as if it were history. "You know how deadly that is?" I asked. Amir nodded agreement. The boy just shrugged again.

"Big ... like I said. That's how I roll."

The kid's all right. He's got that mix of arrogant, reckless, and fragile … reminds me a lot of Robert. I wonder if he plays guitar. If I ever see him again I'll ask.

I glanced over to Amir's drawing. It's pretty damned spectacular, actually. He must be some sort of professional artist, but he hasn't really talked about it. "I draw cuz that's all I can do," he said.

"Do *They* ever bother you?" I asked Amir (we then explained to the white boy who *They* are. He didn't seem too concerned).

"Not really," Amir replied. "I see *Them. They* look at me. But *They* don't ever approach. I think *They* know my walking days are long over."

Pretty much every theory I listed earlier as flat-out bunk Amir apparently believes in one hundred percent, and he's irritated that neither the white boy nor I are buying any of it.

"Believe what you want," he grumbled. "I know what I've seen."

"I have a theory of my own," the white boy snickered. "You see the meteor shower Wednesday night? Well, I think those are really just God rubbing one out."

"Ah yes," I played along. "The great and holy galactic orgasm spurting across the night sky."

"Y'all can both take a hike," Amir replied, not amused.

"I plan to," the white boy said. "I really need to get out of here. Been fun and all, but I've got business in Sacramento '04."

No sooner did he say that when a guard rapped against the bars and pointed at him.

"You. Time to go." The three of us stared at the guard for a moment, waiting for a twitch or a jerk or some indication. Nothing. He appeared clean. Even still I suddenly had a bad feeling about the white boy's walk back.

Apparently Amir felt it to, because he said, "I don't think you should go, son."

"I agree," I said. "Why don't you wait and I'll go with you. No charge. Some of those paths are treacherous, and I know what to look out for."

"Nah," the white boy said. "I'm not too worried about it, honestly. I'll see you guys again sometime. Later." And away he went. I hope he was right.

I asked Amir what he meant by "I know what I've seen." This is his story (I've asked him to speak slowly so I could get it all down):

I was born in Mississippi 1932. When I was a little past one year old my father was lynched. I have no real memory of him ... just an impression of his big, rich voice. There was one photo of him with my mother but I lost it long ago. Someone, I don't know who, decided my mother was unfit to raise me and I was set to be shipped off to Alabama to live with my aunt and uncle. My mother's parents had both died of TB the previous year; my father's parents was long dead. Instead of being sent to Selma, though, I somehow ended up living with my great grandparents in a tiny wood shack in the bayou. Thinking about it now it was a scary place ... our only neighbors was damaged old, sick, people ... but I suppose I was too young to be frightened. Great-grandmama died when I was four, and that was around the time I discovered the pass way. Had I gone to New York City in my own time it would have blown me away, but to see it in 2001 was beyond my imagination. And my great-grandfather, Granddad I called him, God bless his soul, was simply too old and feeble to control me, so I pretty much ran wild on both sides of the pass way. I would periodically go to West Point and watch my mother from afar, resenting her for abandoning me, although I found out later it weren't her doing. When I was six, a man came through from the other side. Freak-looking devil. But that's not so much what bothered me. It was something else about him. One night two Negro men got lynched. One was hanged, the other burned alive. Being my usual curious self, I ran off to see them. There was a crowd gathered when I got there and that man was there too. And as his eyes caught mine I knew he was my father. He was a different man ... different body, different skin, a different man plain and simple. But he was my father. He didn't even know it his own self, but I knew. Not long after that, he was gone. And my mother ran off and disappeared. I think she walked the pass way. I never saw her again. After that I finally was shipped off to Selma and my aunt and uncle raised me. I never walked through time ever again, and I doubt I ever will. But sometimes I think I'd like to try and find her.

"It's not too late," I told him.

"Maybe someday ... " he replied.

"So how do you know that man was your father?" I asked.

"I just know," he said, his southern accent slipping through the cracks. "I just know."

I'm not convinced.

"Is your real name Amir Mwate?"

"Nope," he replied as he finished his drawing by 'signing' the corner with a small face. "*They're* in here," he said, looking about the jail. I'm sure he's right about that.

❄

My Dearest Anna,

By the time you read this, I will be gone. I am so sorry. I know this is a cowardly thing to do, but I ain't lived like no man, so I don't deserve to die like no man. Words can't speak proper the shame I have inside.

I always promised I'd never burden you with the things I done. Always did feel I was doing the right thing, but fact is, I ain't felt that way in a long time. I got to say what I got to say and I know you'll be hurting, but I think that you ought to know it.

Five years ago, that nig Negro man Walter Brown looked up at me dead in the eye, blood pouring off his face, one second from death, and he said to me

This moment. Don't never forget it.

And then we killed him. We killed him. Killed him like we done killed so many others. Don't even know what he done wrong. Don't even know if he done wrong. But he stuck that talk in my head and I ain't shook it from then on. Every time, every moment since, I hear that bouncing round in my mind.

This moment. Don't never forget it.

Anna, I am trapped forever in this moment. Lord forgive me.

Last night, the boy he kept on saying my name. Over and over as we done it. He wouldn't stop.

How many more innocent people you gonna kill, Lennis? How many more innocent people you gonna kill, Lennis? I thought you said you don't lynch your own, Lennis. And then he start laughing. Laughing and laughing. And Fisher called him a nigger.

—Shut up nigger—Fisher said to him, and Hank bashed him with a side of cut lumber.

His eyes was bloodshot, and his nose was smashed, his teeth was knocked in, and he looked right at me, like he could see right through the hood, and said

This moment. Don't never forget it.

And I brung my boot down and I crushed his head in.

I ain't no man, Anna. I ain't no man.

Please Holy God in Heaven have mercy on my wicked soul.

There's a song I heard before. One time I heard Eli sing it. And I know it is an old Negro religion song. It goes
God moves on the water. And the people come run and pray. Maybe at last I'll find my peace at the bottom of the Mississippi. I will always love you, my darling. Please find your smile again someday.

Your loving,
Lennis

Q.

Last thing before I go:

I've just been released. I'm not sure why, but I'm free. The National Guard have overtaken Watts and everything is "under control." Time to be on my way.

As I was being lead out, Amir suddenly jumped up and yelled to me through the bars, "Hey! I remember you now! Don't go to Mississippi! DO NOT GO BACK TO MISSISSIPPI!" Which is probably sage advice in general. I have to think, though, if I can survive Watts these past few days, I can handle anything. I most definitely am going back to Mississippi, but I'll be sure to keep extra careful. I have to go collect my belongings from the Tilsons, then I have to see about closing a deal. West Point, Mississippi 1938. I'm excited to get there. Feels like going home.

DEAR DIARY,

Please God in Heaven show me the way. I ain't got no earthly notion of where I standing right now. It is louder than Hades and crowded and everything moving so fast.

They done killed him again! They killed my baby again! Lord what I done to deserve this? How you going give him back to me then take him again like so? Where your mercy now, Lord? Where your mercy now? Lord o Lord why can't I never leave this pain behind? I am trapped forever in this moment!

I gots with me the bag I packed when he come running into the house saying, We gots to go now, Ella! We gots to go right now! Hellhounds on my trail! he say.

And I grab these here pictures he painted, and my bag, and we run on blind through the night.

Going catch a train!

But we never did catch no train. Headlights was surrounding us. I heard them voices laughing

Nigger, Got you nigger.

We looked for way out, but couldn't see nothing on account of the lights.

Can't run left. Can't run right.

Can't run no way cept for straight on into them woods.

I want you to know, my Love say to me, That it ain't never over! We will be together, matter what. They done tore us apart before, but I always come for you. I always come for you.

Now run! Run fast and find the Wolf! He will take you there!

And I done just that. I run and I run! I heard them mens get on him with sticks and rocks, and I bout to turn round when he say

Don't look back Ella! You just keep on running! Find the Wolf!

And I runnin and runnin and I don't find nobody

but he find me.

Big Foot Chester hiding in the woods, and he say, You gots to come this way, Miss Jessie!

Trapped here forever, Chester, I says to him and I can't help but
cry.

You ain't the onlyest one, Miss Jessie. We is all trapped. Just follow
till you don't see me no more, then just keep on till light. Don't
never stop till light.

Now light done come, and where the Wolf?
Now light done come and gone, and where could I be?

They done killed my baby again O Lord!
Can't never get out this pain. Stuck here. Trapped here. Prisoner
here.
Walking round this here loud city, I seen the building over yonder.
That same brown stone building my baby made the picture of. I
look at the picture and look at the building and it even got them
same numbers on it. I cross over to it and this yellow automobile
come screeching up and I think somebody call me a heifer! I ran
up to the walkway, and I seen this horrible in the back of the auto!
A horrible! Had all colored ropes and such hanging from the head,
and metal pieces in the face.
Face all bloody and screaming Drive you bastard! Drive!
I just set on them steps outside not knowing what.
Not knowing nothing of nothing.

So I walk into this here brown stone building. Up the steps to a open
door. This room ain't like nothing I seen before, Diary. There some
sort a new fangled phonograph with a record album still spinning.
Memphis Minnie. Dirty Mother For You. The walls got all manner of painted pictures every which way. And some of them hold a
likeness to ME cept I be wearing some voodoo-witchdoctor get-up.
God Above, all this got to mean something. What could it be?

There a picture propped up, a sure enough ugly, but it seem to be
not quite done. Look like a hunk of beef screaming bloody murder
with Sleepy Oc wrote on it. Ugly as sin.

On a little table there be a black box with a red shining on and then going off. I done touched the red and a voice come on saying There has been a terrible! and then it made a tiny whistle.
Can't reason none of this.

I finally did get my crying to stop for a spell, Diary. Now what to do? What to do? If I can figure this here phonograph into playing a note or two, reckon I could ease my weary mind. Reckon I could dance a piece. And cry a small bit more as well.
Spose I will just stay in this here place till the Lord show me the way,
or somebody come chasing for me too.

EPILOGUE

"Brothers and Sisters ... "

It is as I write this September 2004, and I find myself stuck within a moment in time. *A Prayer for Dawn* has been out for two months. The full stage play of *Chasing The Wolf* had its world premiere in June. And it's been almost exactly one month since ...

> *I remember sitting by the creek finishing a bottle of wine.*
> *Yeah, high school's gonna be weak, but we'll just do our time.*
>
> *So call me in the morning. There are mountains in need of climbin'.*
> *Though no one likes our jokes, they can't deny our timin'.*

It was around this time, August of 1982, that Simon and I met, beat the living hell out of each other (as boys our age are wont to do), and became best of friends (ditto). And for the next twenty years were pretty much inseparable. Growing up our houses were so close one could easily pelt his back porch with mud balls from my backyard. (Which I did. On multiple occasions. My deepest apologies to whomever lives there now.)

> *I remember sitting by the street finishing a bottle of wine.*
> *Hell yeah this town is weak. But we'll just do our time.*
>
> *So let's write a song or twelve, and do some bullshit rhymin'.*
> *Though no one likes our music, they can't deny our timin' ...*

Simon and I went to grade school, high school, and college together, lived in numerous slummy apartments together, rode in the back seat of police cruisers together, wrote together, played in bands together. The night he left for graduate school at the University of California, Berkeley we considered that it would be the first time in twenty years we'd really be separated. Certainly two grown men could stand to spend at least a little time apart. Indeed.

So yeah, let's posse up. This town is ripe for crimin'.
So folks don't like our jokes, but we got perfect timin'.

For someone who was perpetually late his entire life, Simon was obsessed with time. "How old were we when … " "How old will we be when … " "How old was Soandso when he recorded that song … " "We haven't got a lot of time on this." "Clock's tickin', man. Clock's tickin'." He was always racing against time. Always running up against time. Always fighting against time.
There never would have been enough time.

Hey good night, everybody. This ain't good bye, all right?
We'll call y'all in the morning. Brothers and sisters, good night.

Around the time that the curtain closed on the premiere of *Chasing The Wolf*, Simon was graduating from the Berkeley School of Journalism. Struggling, of course, as always, but there was no doubt that his brilliance, his cunning, his talent, his unbridled imagination, would take him anywhere he wanted to go. No doubt.

Come on, it's morning now …

On August 18th he fell asleep on a friend's couch, and … they say he never felt a thing because he never woke up.
On October 23rd, he would have been 30 years old.
As Kurt Vonnegut might say, so it goes.

Now we're all waiting by the phone … but it just isn't chimin'.
No, we don't like your joke, but you got perfect timin' …

The Wolf

Chasing The Wolf has already had many lives. I hope it has many more. I have over the years performed it in part and as a whole live as a solo act and in small ensembles. Seeing the full cast stage adaptation in May at the Performance Gallery here in Cincinnati was an unparalleled thrill. The performers were all fantastic. The sets, the sound, the direction, the live music ... all wonderful. *I wish Simon could have seen it.* He was the first person to read the original draft of this book. The first to give me notes on it. *Detailed* notes. We talked often as I sweated through the process of adapting the rough version of the novel into the play that it became. He was fascinated by the idea of taking figments of the imagination and turning them into living, breathing characters on stage. So was I. I still am.

So come on, hurry up! Don't lag behind like you do.
We're all just waiting here. Don't make me come collect you.

Had it not been for Simon, I likely would never have even written this story. He was the person who first introduced me to the music of Howlin' Wolf. "You've got to hear this fuckin' guy," he said. "You've never *heard* this voice before." He was right. I hadn't. I'd heard Charlie Patton. I was familiar with Captain Beefheart. But *no one* sounds like Wolf. In his growl, in his howl, his heavy, thunderous guitar riffs, his paranoid ranting, in his wail and his moan, I hear a *thousand* stories. The more I explored, the more I read about the man, his life, his performances, and the more I experienced his music, the more I thought *Goddamn ... this guy was metal when Black Sabbath were in diapers.* As Sam Phillips said the first time he heard Wolf sing, "This is for me. This is where the soul of a man never dies." *Where the soul of a man never dies.* Indeed. I loved that Wolf hadn't recorded until his later years. I loved that Howlin' Wolf as a young man, as he appears in this story, only exists in legend and hearsay and the foggy memories of very old people. Those unreliable, out-of-focus tales are some of my favorites. They are the myths for a culture that has no mythology. There's a scratchy old 78 playing through one ripped speaker on a Victrola down the hall, and I can't quite make out the tune. That is my favorite song.

So come on, hurry up! Don't drag behind like you do.
We're all just waiting here. And we can't leave without you.

I guess *Chasing The Wolf* is my little stab at the legend—the tall tales and the myth-making. It is a song in its own way. A field holler. A swamp moan. The raw shit, Delta-style, tinny and muffled. Scratched up and dirty. A walk down the rocky pass way of time, where the road is dark, and goddamn it if the wind isn't whispering your name. And it sings a little different every time. A blues song ought to. I reckon.

So good night Mom and Dad. This ain't good bye, all right?
I'll call you in the morning. Brothers and sisters, good night.

Blues thrives in contradiction. It is joy and pain. Harsh and soothing. Victim and aggressor. Oppressive and liberating. Arrogant, huge, strutting, larger-than-life, beaten down, dogged, driven, and broken-hearted. Broken-hearted. It is refusing to let go …
and saying goodbye when it's time to say goodbye.

But right now, I prefer a simple *good night.*

So good night, everybody. This ain't goodbye, all right? I'll call you in the morning.

Brothers and sisters, good night.

Nathan Singer, 2004